HE'S SO BAD

A SAN FRANCISCO LOVE STORY

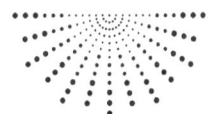

Z.L. ARKADIE

Z.L. ARKADIE BOOKS

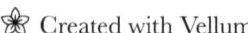

ACKNOWLEDGMENTS

Thanks to the following:
    Edited by Red Adept Editing
    Cover Design by Z.L. Arkadie Books

WHAT SHAME

FIVE MONTHS AGO...

*S**he* moans, and it makes me harder. We're in the supply closet in my New York office, flanked by ballpoint pens, legal pads, staplers, and shit like that. Her stomach is pressed against my drafting table. The edge of a blueprint that I've been working on catches my eye. Drafting is a hobby of mine. When I have nothing to do, which is often, I walk into an old building, imagine how I would rebuild it, then return to this room and sketch my recreation.

"Shush," I whisper to the girl. I don't know her name, but this is the third time I've asked her to keep quiet.

I fuck her type often. She thinks making noises will make me come faster, and that's what she wants. She isn't enjoying the pounding I'm giving her. The way I'm fucking her isn't meant for her enjoyment. It's meant for mine.

She and I have been flirting for a while. She works on the twenty-second floor. Whenever I come to the New York office, we end up riding the elevator together at least three times a week. This morning I broke from the norm and asked if she wanted to see where I worked. She raised an eyebrow and let the door close on the twenty-second floor. The elevator opened on the twenty-third floor, and she followed me out of it. Only a few people were sitting at their desks but not for long. Like everyone else, they were on their way to the large conference room for today's company-wide meeting.

Once in my office, she strutted around my desk, touching shit. "No pictures?"

I was dazed by how her long hair grazed the small of her back. Just beneath was one gorgeous ass just begging to be handled.

"I prefer real life," I said.

She grinned impishly. I had impressed her with my bullshit. The truth is I have nobody to put in a picture frame. My father's dead, and my mom abandoned me for her new husband and the children they have together.

She sat on the edge of my desk and crossed her legs, hiking up her hip. "But a picture's worth a thousand words."

The long muscle that ran up her thigh made my pants tight. I smirked. "How about I show you my favorite part?"

Her eyebrows crumpled. "Favorite part of what?"

"My office."

"Is it this?" She spread her hand over the top of my desk as she batted her eyelashes at me.

I was the spider that had just captured the fly. I nodded toward the supply closet. "It's in there."

I observed the look in her eye as she calculated the risk, wondering if I was the type who would fuck her and forget her. I grinned to sway her thoughts in my favor.

"You have a Jacuzzi in there?" she asked.

I walked boldly to the closet and opened the door. "You want to come and see?"

She hesitated but chose to enter. She stopped in front of my drafting table and turned to face me.

I got close enough to feel her quick breaths

against my chin. "Do you know how long I've been wanting to kiss you?" That line never failed me.

Her lips parted. "How long?"

"This long." I pulled her soft body against me.

I kissed her gently at first. She stared into my eyes. I'd seen that look a million times. She was searching for the promise of dinner tonight and our first stroll as a couple in Central Park this weekend. My expression gave her no answers or false illusions. I wanted to fuck. Apparently she did too because she kissed me back. My dick got harder. She unzipped my pants. I lifted her skirt.

And now my heavy-lidded gaze is pinned to her round ass as I watch my dick shift in and out of her like a locomotive. The sight adds fuel to my fire, and I bang her harder.

"Shit," I mutter. Not because my dick feels good but because she's too inexperienced to know how to chase an orgasm and get the most out of my engorged cock.

I lift her hips about a half inch and aim for the right spots to help her out. She makes a new sound, nothing like the fake squealing noise porn actresses make. I'll be damned if I let her leave this room not knowing that she just experienced the fuck of her life.

Since I've made this morning diversion worth it for her, I can let myself blow. I toss my head back. My balls tighten. Blood rushes to my dick. Then I hear…

"Wait a second, Maggie." It's Mavis.

My office door closes. I put a hand over the chick's mouth and lean over to put my lips to her ear. "Hush," I whisper.

"Take your hand off my mouth," the woman hisses.

She stands straight, and my deflated dick falls out of her. I put my fingers across my lips, asking her to remain silent. She rolls her eyes defiantly but complies nevertheless.

"Is Robert there?" Maggie asks. She's on speaker.

"You know he never shows up for the weekly meeting. Hell, he hardly shows up for work."

"Is that still the case?"

"We actually get more done when he's not here anyway. Vince has been using me as his New York assistant."

"Oh, so you work with Langley?" That's Vince's regular assistant.

"Yeah, but jeez, Maggie, I'm over being his assistant. He's just not my cup of tea."

I ignore the way the girl from the elevator looks at me as if she's trying to assess whether or not I'm the asshole they're talking about.

"But he pays you an executive's salary," Maggie says.

"Which is only because he was fucking with you." Mavis sighs. "He's such a game player. And do you know what else I hate about Tango?"

"That he looks at your ass and pussy like he's a starving hyena?" Maggie says.

Mavis laughs a little. "Yes. That. I feel like he has fucked me a million times in his imagination. To him, women are pussies, not people. I think his greatest ambition is to get trapped in a porno."

Maggie laughs so loud that it sounds as if she's in the closet. "Thanks, Mavis, I needed that."

Mavis chuckles. "Well, it's true. The way he looks at women is disgusting, and may I say sad."

The chick I was fucking meets my gaze. She's heard the awful truth about me, and so have I.

"Yeah, well… give him a break. Robert is only a lost soul because Vince has done a mighty fine job of enabling him," Maggie says.

Suddenly I feel ashamed of myself. They're discussing me as if I'm a cross between a hormonal teenager and a dirty old man.

"It's pathetic," Mavis says.

"I don't know. Someday Robert will be forced to pull his head out of Vince's ass and figure out what the hell he was put on this earth to do—"

"Other than chase skirts," Mavis says snidely.

"Right…" Maggie sighs as if the thought of me getting my shit together is a long and arduous plight. "But enough talk about him. I'm happy to have you back in my universe."

"I've already typed up my two weeks' notice," Mavis says.

I close my eyes to endure the brunt of the distressing emotions surging through me. My fuck buddy straightens her skirt. Before over-hearing Mavis and Maggie's conversation, she probably believed she was fucking a mighty man; now she knows she's been nailed by a mouse.

Her face has turned red, and she's fanning herself. "I have to go." She starts for the door, puffing as if she can't catch her breath.

I reach out to stop her. "Please…"

But she's too quick.

Mavis gasps. "What the hell?"

My heart beats a mile a minute as I listen to the main door open then slam shut. What was supposed to have been a ten-minute dose of pussy has turned into a disaster.

I zip my pants. "Shit, shit, shit…" I put on a brave face and walk into the office, determined to carry the shame like a man.

Mavis's mouth falls open. With her low opinion of me, I'm surprised she's shocked. My heart is beating even faster. I tighten my jaw as my eyes water. I've never quite felt like this before. It feels like I've been sentenced to eternal damnation or some shit.

"What's the matter?" Maggie says.

Mavis and I look at the cell phone, which she's put on my desk. I think part of her stunned expression comes from being caught taking some liberties inside my office. It's not like her to do that. She always asks if she can sit down, open this or that, or walk through my office to get to the supply cabinet.

"Nothing," Mavis says spastically. "I'll call you later."

"Is everything okay?" Maggie asks.

"Everything is fine," she says, more composed.

"Doesn't sound like it."

"Well, it is. I just have to take another call."

Maggie pauses. "Okay then."

Mavis watches me with panicked eyes. "Talk to you later."

"Later."

Maggie hangs up, and Mavis swipes her phone off my desk. "Sorry." She looks from my face to the supply closet. I wish I had closed the door. "Um…"

I'm so fucking embarrassed. All I can do is drop my face, clear my throat, and say, "You don't have to wait." I lift my head.

Mavis can't look me in the eyes. "I'm so sorry for invading your space."

I wave off her apology and massage my temple. "You don't need to give me a two weeks' notice."

Mavis presses a hand to her chest. "Oh… you heard that. I'm so sorry. I didn't mean… I mean…" She drops her face and shakes her head.

Her demeanor baffles me. She appears remorseful, which is a one-hundred-eighty degree turn from her earlier opinion of me. I would respect her more if she would show me the truth of how she feels about me. I don't say a word. Instead I glare at her until she finds the will to look me in the eyes. Finally she does.

"You can go," I say.

She still looks confused.

Rage mixed with the incessant need to be alone fills me. "Two weeks! I'll pay you! Go!"

Mavis jumps. "I didn't mean to…"

Her worried expression gets to me, and I take the asshole out of my expression. "Go work for Maggie. I wish you the best."

Mavis parts her lips. Damn, they're sexy. I feel disgusting for wanting to kiss her and fuck her. I suddenly realize that it isn't Mavis I want to pound —not all of her at least. I don't want to fuck her personality or emotions. I just see tits, ass, curves, and pussy. I look away from her and rub my temples because my head hurts.

"But I can work for two more weeks or however long you need me."

I shake my head. "Just go."

She's still there. Her presence washes over me like an ice-cold tidal wave.

"I'll just get my stuff," she finally says.

I listen to her heels click against the floor. Her steps are slow and unsure. I'm a blob of mixed emotions, stuck here and staring out the window. Am I the sorry asshole that Vince has been carrying on his back for all of these years?

I think back to three ago, before Maggie showed up at A&Rt Media. Vince and I had a system. He ran the show, and I looked after the money by meeting with Gabe Zenith, our accountant, once a week. Our sit-downs consisted of us shooting the breeze for ten minutes. Next Gabe would run down the financial gains report. I would only cut in to ask him to be more specific about how the money got from point A to point B. Our meetings always culminated with him informing me that financially, A&Rt Media was in a great position. That was what I reported back to Vince. I figured I would spare him the details.

I recall the time he patted me on the back and said, "Great." Was he patronizing me? Whenever Vince insisted I attend an event or meeting to show myself as a figurehead or when he called me into his office to sign business-oriented documents, I complied. Sometimes, while in the moment, I found my CEO requirements belittling. These days, the scope of my involvement with A&Rt business has changed. I tried my hand at launching a new show for Prime D TV but failed. My dick was in it more than my heart was. I had something going on with Hannah Brady, the producer of a show I was trying to get off the ground. Neither ended well.

I look toward the gentle rapping on my door. It's a woman's knock.

I clear my throat. "Yes." That sounded good —composed.

"I'm leaving," Mavis says without opening the door.

"Good luck," I say.

She pauses. "The same to you."

I sit and wait until she's good and gone before I grab my briefcase and get the hell out of Dodge before the big morning meeting ends.

Two Hours Later...

I JUST FINISHED my walk through the Carlyle. Whenever I feel like shit, I visit my favorite buildings in the city. The Carlyle Hotel is one of them. A&Rt Media keeps an apartment here for upscale guests who come to town for a meeting or a visit. The lease is in my name. If I were ever to part ways with the company, then the apartment would go to me. I skip down the marble staircase. I've spent an hour overdosing on Roaring Twenties lavishness. I've reimagined this hotel at least fifty different ways, and none of my reinventions kept the hotel looking close to the way it is now.

I exit the building through the lobby. The extra light makes me squint. It's September and a comfortable seventy degrees or so, but I'm sweating like a pig as I walk south on 3rd Avenue. There's a bar about ten blocks away. My first inclination is to stop and drink whisky until I forget this shitty day ever happened, but I need more than a round of stiff drinks to take the edge off. I need a warm, soft body. I need pussy. The women don't trickle into the bar until after five.

I've been stopped by a red light. There's a pretty blonde across the street. She's wearing tight jeans, a low-cut sheer blouse, and high heels. A big leather bag, one of those expensive ones, hangs on her arm. Cars and buses whisk by. The woman is thinner than I like, but I leer at her anyway.

Someday Robert will be forced to pull his head out of Vince's ass and figure out what the hell he was put on this earth to do… Maggie says inside my head. *Other than chase skirts*, Mavis replies.

The stoplight turns green. The blonde has noticed me watching her, and she cracks a tiny smile. The herd of pedestrians around me rushes across the street. The girl bats her eyelashes. I have a second to make a decision. I can expand my smirk, say hello, and ask her if she has a second.

She'll say yes, and I'll walk with her. This time, I'll ask for her name and where she's from. She'll ask the same of me.

"Are you on your way to the office?" I would ask in a tone that indicates there's no motive behind that crucial question.

If she says yes, then I'd be forced to take her number and decide whether it's beneficial to call her later—in this case, it would not be. If she says no, then I would ask her for a cup of coffee and conversation. She'd play hesitant, but after one good head-to-toe look at me, she'd give in to my minimal powers of persuasion.

Most men couldn't pull off picking up a woman so easily, but I could. My suit is Brioni. My shoes are Mezzomi, a little-known but brilliant Italian designer who handcrafts each shoe. Basically, I look and smell expensive. The woman has already fantasized about introducing me to her single friends, making them jealous in the process. And this chick is no Pollyanna. She can tell a good fuck when she sees one, and she's already sussed me out. Engaging with this attractive woman is certainly one way to go.

However, I see myself standing alone, facing down the fork in the road. One path leads to self-destruction, and the blonde is the first person I'll encounter.

The blonde and I pass each other. The glimmer in her eyes and the tiny smile make it clear she's trying to seduce me. But I nod and look forward. I have no fucking idea what's down the other path, but I choose to walk it even though it scares the hell out of me. I have forsaken the pussy. That's definitely a road that I've never taken, but now that I'm on it, I can say that it feels like the path to salvation.

2

THE END OF AN ERA

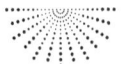

Yesterday, after I crossed the street, I went home. I spent the rest of the day and night sitting on the sofa in my living room, staring out over the city lights. Even when I became sleepy, I forced my eyes to stay open and my brain to keep thinking. I needed answers. I needed to make changes, life-altering ones, which meant I had to break through some serious mental barriers. Sweat drenched my skin. At times, I got up and paced until what felt like hours had passed. I fought the urge to sift through my contact list within the STAT (Sure Thing—stat) folder and call up a nice piece of ass.

I fuck a lot. I like to fuck. But when the fucking

is over, I'm alone, and I'm not sure if I'm the guy who likes being alone.

However, I'd pushed through, battling my fears, anxiety, and shit like that. If Vince had enabled me, then I needed to empower myself. By daybreak, the answer was as clear as a light at the end of the tunnel.

I rub my eyes; they're tired and burning. I want to crash, but I have work to do. I call Gabe Zenith and let him know that I want to divest myself of A&Rt Media. According to my contract, I'm obligated to offer Vince the opportunity to purchase my interest in the company for fifty percent of the value of my shares, and I need Gabe to orchestrate the transfer.

Gabe's silent for a while. "Are you sure?"

I had pondered the answer to that question until I was blue in the face. My friendship with Vince has always been dysfunctional as hell, but it didn't have to end up this way. I'm the one at fault. I remember that spiel Maggie gave me about wanting to play with Vince's toys, not because his toys were shinier or prettier but because Vince had enjoyed them. I pictured myself as a ruddy-faced kid, the biggest brat on the planet, stealing my best friend's shit. Deep inside, all this kid wants is to steal his brother's happiness. My fucking envy made me commit the biggest infraction against my friend. And what the hell did I get out of fucking Maggie? The sex wasn't even as memorable as I thought it would be. Point blank, I don't want to be that kid anymore. If Vince ever forgives me, and I know one day he will, then I want him to do it looking me in the eyes, man to man, not fucking brat to man.

"I'm positive," I say.

Gabe takes a long sigh. "Once you do this, there's no going back."

"I said I'm positive."

I can hear the warning in his silence. The friction between Vince and me has hit Gabe over the head like a wrecking ball. Gabe is another person who believes I'll end up pissed in an alley if Vince stops babysitting me.

"Gabe, I'll be fine," I say.

"Okay, then. I'll be in touch."

The call ends. I close my eyes and feel the weight of what I just did. Gabe was right—there's no going back. And even if I want to run and hide under Vince's wing, he'll just crush me unless I prove to him that I'm incapable of crossing him ever again. I get up and stretch. It's finally time to shit, shower, and shave, and hopefully get enough sleep to get rid of this throbbing headache.

SEVEN HOURS LATER...

I'm back in my midtown office, waiting for Vince and Gabe to show up with the finalized contracts. They'll be here soon. The sale price is 2.3 billion dollars. Vince has already transferred the balance to my bank account. He's not fucking around. He's glad I'm out, and that hurts like hell. Once this is over, I'll fly to Tahiti or somewhere to lick my wounds and plan my next step.

There's a rap on the door. I sit up straight. My heart pounds like a jackhammer. "Come in." I'm surprised to see Jack Lord walk into my office.

"Glad I caught you before you left," he says.

I relax my shoulders. "Then you heard."

He puts a hand on the back of the chair across from mine. "May I?"

"Please." I'm not surprised Jack Lord asked if he could sit. Most men of his stature wouldn't, but he's a rare mix of civility and shrewdness. Vince knows the business of media, but Jack? He writes the rules on the business of business.

"Of course I heard," Jack says.

I press my lips together.

"So what next?" he asks.

That's the question I toiled over until the day broke and the answer came. I throw up my hands casually. "I think I'll try my hand at architecture. It's what I know more about than this."

Jack crosses his legs and grins as he nods.

I narrow an eye curiously. "What is it?"

"I was hoping you'd say that. You've been looking at blueprints for my projects and revising them for the longest time. You've given me valuable advice, Rob."

I shrug indifferently. "I didn't consider it anything more than a favor."

"It was more than a favor. I paid those fuckers a lot of cash to have you fix their fuck-ups."

I don't know how to respond to that. I haven't been praised for my work since my three-year apprenticeship under Barney Arsenault of Customize Designs. For some fucking reason, after graduating from college with a dual degree in architecture and marketing, I came to the conclusion that architecture wasn't prestigious enough. Now that I look back, I was competing with Vince, who had plans to build a media empire with or without me. With all the money he was destined to make, I didn't want him to leave me in the dust, so I exhausted the earnings from my trust fund and invested in Vince's dreams.

Jack ruffles his eyebrows. "You're licensed, aren't you?"

"Passed the test on the first take." I'm pretty proud about that. Not many pass the test the first time and with flying colors.

"Then it's time for me to pay you back," he says.

I frown inquisitively.

"I know you've heard of Ralph Kennedy," Belmont says.

The mention of that name makes me sit up and throw all of my attention at Jack. "He owns a firm in San Francisco. It was one of the top architecture firms in the eighties and nineties."

"He's selling. Are you interested?"

"He's selling? Why?"

Jack shrugs. "I think it's money issues, but they won't confirm it. Instead they're saying he's ready to retire."

"And you don't buy it?"

"No. The shit doesn't add up."

I tap my fingers on my soon-to-be-old desk as I consider Jack's suggestion. Running my own firm would be scary as hell. But what are the odds that this opportunity would present itself at this point in time? I never believed fate could work on my behalf, but it feels like it probably has.

I lean against the back of my office chair. Finally I feel as though I can fit its executive-size largeness. "Hell, I'm interested."

Jack winks. "Good."

I keep a confident look on my face even though I'm losing my shit. "Thanks, Jack."

He leaps to his feet. "Don't thank me yet, Tango. Kennedy is being selective about who he sells his company to, but I have the inside line."

I stand to shake his hand, struggling to maintain my confidence. Why in the hell would Kennedy sell his baby to a man with no working experience in the field? I wouldn't sell to me. Jack seems to be reading my mind, but just as he's about to say something, Vince and Gabe walk into my office. Vince regards me with a stern expression then quickly looks at Jack.

"Are you sitting in on this?" he asks Jack.

Jack waves dismissively. "What for?"

Vince flops down in the seat Jack just abandoned. "Then we'll talk later."

Jack reminds me to expect a call later. Vince

seems mildly curious, but he doesn't relax that frown. He wants me to experience the chill, and he doesn't have to worry, because I feel every inch of it. Gabe pulls up an extra chair to sit beside Vince. He takes the contract out of his messenger bag, puts the stack on my desk, and goes right into explaining the particulars of the sale.

The tension in the room is suffocating as hell. I loosen my tie as I try to look Vince in the eyes, but he's avoiding mine. Although it was my idea to sell him my interest in the company, I'm kind of surprised he didn't try to talk me out of it. He used to love me, but now he fucking hates me. Things haven't been good between us for months. Vince is the king of delayed reactions. In the back of my mind, I knew he would never forgive me if I fucked Maggie, but I did it anyway. I can't imagine why I went through with banging her. I probably need a shrink to figure it out, but what's done is done.

Gabe presses his finger against a plastic tab. "Sign here, Robert."

I pause to give Vince the chance to stop me. I wouldn't change my mind, but it would be nice to know he gave a damn. But he makes it clear that I won't get what I want, so I sign. Gabe flips through the thick stack of documents, directing me where to put my John Hancock. Each scribble makes me feel as if the wind has been knocked out of me. In about ten seconds, I'll be 2.3 billion dollars richer but one friend, my best friend, poorer.

"And here," Gabe says.

We reach the final page. My eyes meet Vince's glare. Shit, I think I'm heartbroken. I'm waiting for him to say, "Stop, don't, let's talk this out." The longer we stare into each other's eyes, the more evident it becomes that I'm dead to him. He looks as if he's viewing my cold dead body lying still in a coffin. I sign.

Gabe swipes up the papers. "That's it. Deal done."

Vince stands. "Good luck, Rob." He turns his back and walks out before I can stand to meet him.

Gabe looks from Vince to me with a frown. He seems very aware that our friendship, which spanned so many years that I stopped counting them, is dead. Finally Gabe hangs his messenger bag on his shoulder. "Good luck, Robert. Call me if you ever need anything."

"Thank you, I will," I say, although I know he doesn't really mean it. It's as if Vince and I have just gotten a divorce and he gets Gabe in the settlement, but we shake anyway.

Gabe purses his lips and walks out with tension in his mouth. I'm alone, and the solitude comes crashing down on me like a raging tidal wave. I frown at my desk. It dawns on me that this is it. It's over, and I'm a free agent.

My cell phone sounds in my pocket, momentarily dissolving the loneliness. "Hello?"

"Listen, I just spoke to Kennedy. He wants to meet with you tomorrow morning at nine thirty at his office." It's Jack.

I can hardly believe what I'm hearing. "In San Francisco?"

"Yes."

That was fast. I'm overwhelmed by the possibility that Kennedy might sell his operation to someone like me.

Then two men walk into my office with a gray cart. The tall gangly one pulls the cart from the front and the short one with glasses guides it from the back. I've heard about these two guys. Around here, they're called the FU-Crew. Vince sends them out after someone has been fired, let go, or quits to collect the newly departed person's computer and telephone so that they can look at the history of use. They also clear files out of the dearly departed's desk and filing cabinets. It's Vince's way of checking to see if his former employees have been consorting with A&Rt Media's competition. It finally dawns on me that Vince is treating me like he does everyone else. If I had any hope that he would ring me up one day in the near future and say, "Hey, Rob, things are going great with Mags and me, so let's let bygones be bygones," well, it's all gone now.

"I'll be there," I say to Jack.

I end the call and give the FU-Crew entrance into the office to allow Vince and his henchman to officially F-Me.

3

THE PROPOSITION

I arrived in San Francisco last night. After I left A&Rt Media, I went home, packed a suitcase, and took the first available flight from Kennedy to SFO. I have a home in Napa Valley, so I rented a car for one week and told the rep that I'd rent it for longer if need be. Then I put my suitcase in the car and made the hour and a half drive to Napa. When I arrived, I expected to see cobwebs hanging on the walls and dust piled on the roof, but everything was just as I'd left it. I sent a message to my regular cleaning service and thanked them for staying on top of things.

Before my flight, Jack's assistant had emailed me the prospectus and financials for the last ten years on Kennedy Creative. I wasn't sure how he'd gotten his hands on the documents, but I was glad he did. I started reading the material on the airplane before I fell asleep, when the lack of sleep from the previous night caught up to me.

In my house in Napa, I take my shoes off, make myself some coffee, and read some more. I replay the numbers in my head as I slog down the stairs to the subterranean level where one of the master bedrooms opens to a view of downtown. Not even two cups of strong black coffee can battle my fatigue. I take a deep breath and flop down at the head of the bed. The switch to open the automatic blinds is on the wall. I flip it, the blinds roll up, and the small town comes into view. I don't know why, but it relaxes me. I unbutton my shirt, take it off, and kick off my shoes. As I get comfortable on the bed, exhaustion sets in. I close my eyes, and before I know it, I'm lying on my side, and the night beyond the floor-to-ceiling windows has changed to day.

I sit up. "Shit."

I forgot to set an alarm. I pull my phone out of my pants pocket. It's 7:37 a.m. My appointment with Ralph Kennedy is at nine thirty. An angel must be lounging on my shoulder because I didn't over-sleep, and at least for the moment, my head isn't cluttered either.

I take a shower and try not to think about what's to come. There's a high probability that my reputation as Vince's lapdog will convince Kennedy to sell to a more worthy buyer. Regardless, I dry off and suit up. There's no food in the refrigerator, and I have no time to grab a bite to eat before the meeting. I figure I'll have a ton of time to eat after Kennedy laughs me out the building. I'll grab Indian food in the marina.

I want to ride the Harley I keep covered in the garage, but I don't want to wrinkle my suit under my riding jacket, so I drive the car I rented. I'll buy a new one for myself if I have to remain in the area. It's a nice day in Napa. The air is so lax that I want to swim in it. Traffic on the 121 Freeway isn't good, but I take in the rolling green hills, acres of grapevines, and the leaves of stout trees draped over lonely trails.

I haven't been able to get the numbers from the financial reports out of my head. The asking price is six hundred million dollars, but they've only grossed 250 million in the last three years and less than that during previous years. Vince relegated me to the financials for A&Rt Media not only to give me something to do so that I could stay out of his way but also because I've always been good at connecting the dots. There's a connection between man-hours, projects, and financial intake. I'm well aware that no one in their right mind would pay so much for a company that might go bust without Kennedy at the helm. My thoughts shift to the client list.

Traffic is sluggish across the Bay Bridge. I loosen my collar and glance at the clock. I have thirty minutes to get to Grant Avenue and the Embarcadero. I focus on the city rising in the horizon. The answer to the overinflated asking price is on the tip of my tongue. I keep chugging along, and I arrive at my destination with five minutes to spare. I find a parking space, cut the engine off, and sit still in order to collect my bearings. I'm still not sure I want to go through with this. I close my eyes, praying for a sign. Suddenly I'm jolted by the loud revving of a motorcycle engine. My eyes pop open. That did it. I hop out the car with a new spring in my step and head off to meet one of the world's greatest architects.

THE OFFICES ARE in a glass half-dome-shaped structure that sits on a square concrete block surrounded by four tall glass buildings. The structure is in the middle of a grass park and has the only ground view of the marina. I think Ralph Kennedy had a hand in designing the building back in the late eighties/early nineties. He was definitely a master of his era.

When I make it inside the building, there are no signs of life, other than the lingering smell of freshly brewed coffee. I walk down a long hallway that has a glass window on one side and a white wall on the other. Portraits of landmark buildings hang on the wall. One of them is a mounted copy of an expertly drafted blueprint; it's signed by Ralph Kennedy. I make it to the end of the hallway and turn the corner. After a few feet of much the same, I end up in an open-air room full of people sitting at work-stations comprised of high desks and chairs, each surrounded by five-foot-high white laminate cubes. Lots of eyes are on me. Normally I don't mind being the center of attention, but not in this case. Glass-walled offices surround the room. I walk toward the back because I have no idea where the hell to go.

"Excuse me, sir," a woman says from behind me.

I turn and look down at a tiny brunette with

hazel eyes. She's cute, and I automatically check whether or not she's wearing a ring—she is.

"Are you Mr. Tango?" she asks.

"Yes, I am."

She smiles, and her tiny face lights up. I would normally flirt with her at this point, ring or no ring, but I can't forget what Maggie and Mavis think of me. I don't want to be that guy. So instead of showing her my normal smile, I make it tight-lipped and professional.

"I have an appointment with Mr. Kennedy." I dig the way I sounded. That came out perfectly.

"Yes," she sings. "This way."

She walks lightly on her toes as she leads me down a line of desks. I don't look to see who's watching me, but I know I'm still being examined. I feel as if an alien has invaded my body and changed my rules of engagement. The high tables and the smell of lead and drafting paper invigorate me. Many firms use a digital application called CAD for drafting, but I love smelling that many of the architects here are still doing it the old way as well—with a pencil, drafting paper, and a steady hand. Suddenly I want this more than I did before I walked into the building. I want to own this scene.

I lock eyes with Ralph Kennedy, who stands

behind his desk. He's just as I remembered him—a full head of white hair, tanned skin, and naturally scowling eyes. Regardless of his narrowed eyes, I've always known him to be an even-tempered guy who's quicker to laugh than bark, but this morning, he's watching me like a hawk. The young woman ushers me into the office.

"Thank you, Zoe," Ralph says.

Zoe says, "You're welcome," and grins from ear to ear as she closes the door on her way out.

I extend my hand. "Good morning, Mr. Kennedy." I smile without showing teeth. It's important to maintain an air of shrewdness when negotiating business deals.

"Good morning, and just call me Ralph." His handshake is as firm as mine. "How about we go over there and have a seat?"

"All right then, Ralph." I follow his lead and sit in the black leather club chair across from him. I loosen my shoulders to relax.

His green khakis and plaid shirt are impeccable. Ralph crosses his legs. His brown shoes are a high grade of leather. "You come highly recommended by Jack Lord."

I sit my foot on top of my knee in ploy to

convince him that I'm just as confident as he is. "I'm grateful for it."

He rubs his chin and watches me with narrowed eyes. "You should be, because when Jack Lord talks, I listen."

He's conveying an important message without saying a lot. I know Jack is their major client, and I get a sense that Ralph is hoping I fuck this up so that he can report to Jack that I'm clearly not the man to run his company. Ambivalence sets in. I drop my foot off my knee. I know what I want to say, but a young woman with short dark hair walks past the office carrying a motorcycle helmet. Our eyes meet, but she quickly looks away and picks up her pace. That felt like déjà vu, or maybe I've actually seen her before.

"Are you easily distracted?" Ralph asks.

Shit. My eyes shoot back to his face. It's clear that my reputation has preceded me. Something about seeing that young woman dissolved my ambivalence, and I want the whole enchilada that Ralph is selling.

"No. I'm here because I want to buy your company," I say.

"But why? You're no one in my business."

That sounded like a jab, but I don't take it personally. "I have the cash."

"All the prospective buyers have the cash, plus a lot more experience than you."

I shrug cockily, but I'm putting on an act. "I can't argue against either of those points. I've been reviewing and revising Jack's blueprints for a while." I shift in my seat to sit taller. "Remember the Howard Rogers building in Manhattan?"

Ralph shifts in his seat. He's uncomfortable. His lips are moving, but no words come out. Kennedy Creative was hired to design the building, and the architect drafted a plan that would've never worked. Ralph nods in a way that says he's taking ownership of the mistake. "That was one we missed."

"One miss would've been all it had taken if that building had gone up as designed. The library wouldn't have been able to support the weight of the sixteen floors above it."

Ralph strokes his chin with his thumb. "Right…" He shoots to his feet. "Robert, what are you doing tonight?"

I'm caught off guard by his abrupt movement. I stand to meet him. In negotiations, one should never take the inferior position. "I have no plans."

"How about you come over? My wife is having a gathering tonight."

I fold my arms in front of me. "Are you planning on making it worth my while?"

He cracks a tiny smile—the first since we've shaken hands. "You smoke cigars?"

"If the occasion calls for it."

"Then come. I'll have a proposition for you." He opens the door.

I stand still and extend my sense of hearing out the door. The hum of voices, clicking keyboards, pencils running across paper, and life in general flows into the office. It could all be mine—no partners, no Vince. This is the first time in my life that I've felt like an adult man—and it feels fucking incredible.

My lips pull into a slow-forming smile. "What's the address?"

Ralph looks out the window and waves his fingers. Zoe jumps to her feet and prances over like a trained poodle. Her smile is so intense that her eyes narrow to slits.

"Mr. Tango needs details about dinner tonight," Ralph says.

"Great," Zoe says, still smiling. "Mr. Tango, can you please follow me?"

I nod as Ralph sits back down in his executive-size chair. Just for a second, I see him differently. Although his clothes are impeccable, he's frail. Now that I'm in Zoe's hands and he doesn't have to perform for me, there's a faraway look in his eyes.

I follow Zoe to her desk, and she hands me an invitation card. "This has the address, time, and dress code, but what you're wearing now is fine." She stares into my eyes as if she's looking to discover some deep dark secret.

I smile lazily. "Thank you."

We watch each other for a moment. She hasn't relaxed her smile yet. Is she really that happy? I'm not envious and I'm not revolted either, but I surely can't look at that pasted-on smile all day long. If I buy this company, then Zoe will be the first to be reassigned.

"Is that all?" I ask.

I didn't think her smile could grow any wider, but it just did. "Yes!"

I snicker. "Thanks, Zoe."

As soon as I turn to walk off, I catch sight of the woman who walked past Ralph's office while carrying a motorcycle helmet. Her space is across the room, situated in a dark corner. She's concentrating on whatever she's doing at her desk.

"You're welcome, Mr. Tango," Zoe says.

I contemplate asking Zoe for the woman's name but think better of it. I'm careful about the shit I do these days. I don't want to be the same Robert Tango that Mavis and Maggie found so revolting. It's not that I have a sexual attraction toward the motorcycle woman. Hell if I know what I find so alluring about her.

I show Zoe a thumbs-up and continue on my way.

Motorcycle woman doesn't pay the slightest bit of attention to me, which is strange, because everyone else is paying the kind of attention one does to a possible new owner of the firm. Regardless, I head back to my car and drive downtown to the St. Regis hotel. I'd be a fool to drive an hour back to Napa only to return to the city during rush-hour traffic. Once I'm settled in a presidential suite, I take off my suit and call to have it pressed for this evening.

I stretch out on top of the bed and stare at the ceiling. I fight the urge to riffle through my contacts list and call up some company for tonight. For two nights, I've felt like shit and hadn't been able to use sex to soothe me. I think about Zoe's cute little ass, but the possibility of hearing her squeal doesn't turn me on. Plus she's married. Poor guy. Motorcycle woman had a nice ass too, but I don't want to think about her in a sexual way. I don't want to think about her at all.

I know four women I can call. Before, I would pick one and invite her over for dinner provided by room service. I would seduce her until we were fucking, and an hour before leaving for Ralph's dinner party, I would tell her to leave and promise to call her tomorrow. That would be a lie. Most women needed the promise of something more in order to feel good about a fast fuck.

"Why the fuck do I need a body?" I whisper. Why can't my fucking hand suffice?

I flip onto my side and stare out the large window at the view of the city. What the hell do I want out of life other than to purchase Kennedy Creative? Before my father died, I knew the answer. I was eleven years old and in sixth grade when the school principal called me out of class and into the nurse's office. The nurse sat me on the examination table. I was scared as hell, wondering if I was going to get a shot or something, and if so, then what for? But she gave me a lollipop instead. The nurse kept patting me on the back and telling me that everything would be fine. When my mother arrived, as soon as she saw me, she started bawling and held me tightly.

She kept repeating, "Daddy's dead."

At first I didn't know what the entire production meant. My mother always had a flair for the dramatic, and she and my dad were always fighting about one thing or another. I remember her accusing him of cheating all the time. My dad would just look at her, shake his head, and say, "I'm not going to argue with you in front of my son." I always felt as if he was the only person in the world who gave a damn about me, and that made me feel safe and protected.

My memories of that morning are still vivid. My mother's sweet perfume was so strong that it made me loopy. Her thin body crushed me as I watched the principal, Ms. Shine, say to the nurse, whose name eludes me, "He fell off a ladder and broke his neck." She shook her head, pitying me. I'm not sure if the pity was for my father's death or for being the son of a woman who was making a spectacle out of herself.

We dressed in black and went to a funeral. I remember seeing my dad lying in a casket. I thought he was asleep and hoped at any second, he would open his eyes and wake up. At the cemetery, two men rolled the crane to lower the coffin into the ground, and that was when I finally fully comprehended the notion of death. I've never seen my mom happier than when receiving condolences.

After that, I spent a lot of nights at Vince's house while my mother dolled herself up and went out to the local bar. Not even three months later, she was dating Burt, who she eventually married. He was an asshole who drank a lot and fucked around on her. Once, in a drunken state, he told me about how when grizzlies and lions take a mate that already has kids, they kill the little bastards. Then he messed up my hair, laughed, and said, "I'll let you live."

I told Vince what he said. Ann, Vince's mother, was lurking in the hallway and overheard me. She made a lunch date with my mother, and after that, for an entire year, I spent more time at the Adams' house than I did my own. Then my mother divorced Burt, and I stayed home more but spent the entire summer with the Adams at their family vacation house in Sag Harbor. Vince's family was no Brady Bunch, but they weren't half as fucked up as my mother and whichever husband she was married to for the moment. My mom already has five divorces under her belt.

I can't rest, so I sit on the side of the bed. I'm disturbed by the thought that I may not know how to live a normal existence without Vince. I order coffee service and watch the afternoon news for a few hours. The woman with the motorcycle helmet keeps invading my thoughts. There's something about the shape of her face, eyes, and lips.

By six thirty, the laundry service knocks on the door to return my shoes and suit. Both articles are fresh and ready for another wear. I put them on and head out. I'll stay the night and drive back to Napa in the morning.

Valet brings my car, and I put Ralph Kennedy's address into the GPS. San Francisco is an old city. The natives have been dogmatic about preserving the historical architecture, but the landscape has changed ever since the technological boom. Techies like new shit, and they're the new kings of the city. Both factors make me grin from ear to ear. There's some merit in being on the ground floor of giving the old San Francisco a facelift.

The night is breezy, and the air is tepid. I roll down the front windows. The closer I get to the ocean, the saltier the air smells. Ralph lives in the Sea Cliff neighborhood, but the mansions I pass don't excite me. They're mostly Victorian and

Edwardian with sprinkles of Spanish colonial; the neighborhood smells of old money. I don't have an aversion to old money though. Unlike new money, they have a lot of class and knowledge of how to keep their assets and make them grow.

I'm not surprised when the GPS instructs me to turn into the long driveway of the best-looking mansion on the street. It's a Spanish Colonial. The bowl-shaped stone fountain stands out in the middle of a manicured lawn and trimmed shrubs.

A valet station is set up in front of a flagstone footpath. I leave my car with the attendant, and he directs me up a path and through an enclosed and intimate courtyard with red rose bushes woven through the gate. The red brick groundwork stops in front of a steep set of white limestone steps. I take them up to the front door. I'm impressed by a door made of white frosted glass and decorative black wrought iron twisted into the shape of vines and roses. The top part of the door is open, and I hear laughter and conversation. It sounds as though a lot of guests are present.

I hit the doorbell. The button lights up, but there isn't a chime. I've seen this sort of silent doorbell before. A few seconds later, a guy dressed in a black suit with a white shirt appears.

"Welcome, sir," he says. "May I have your name?"

I tell him my name. He nods once and opens the gate. I straighten my collar as I follow him inside. My gaze rolls around the open floor plan. It's furnished just as I thought it would be—fancy furniture, expensive fixtures, and exotic figurines.

I've been smothering my nervousness since this afternoon, and now it's gushing back in a raging tidal wave. The butler, who has made sure he remained three steps ahead of me, stops before reaching the entrance of a dining room where the other guests are seated at one long table.

"Mr. Robert Tango," the butler announces.

After a quick count, I ascertain that there are about thirty people present. The chatter quiets, and all eyes are on me. They look interested to know my story. I'm used to moments like this. I muster up some bravado and crack a smile. I search for Ralph Kennedy among the faces. He makes it easier to find him when he stands.

"Robert, glad you could make it." He gestures at an empty chair across from his. "Have a seat. Our special guest has arrived."

I search the table for other empty seats. The one Ralph pointed me to is situated between two attractive women—one blond and one brunette. The way the women are looking at me makes me nervous. So far I've contained my animal instincts.

"We don't bite," the brunette says, batting her eyelashes.

I'm nervous as hell, but I walk over to sit between the two women. The scent of their perfume and the warmth of feminine energy overtake me.

The pretty brunette on my left, who said she doesn't bite, extends a hand. "I'm Chantal."

I analyze her smile. I'm not sure if she's just being friendly or if she's flirting. I shake her hand. "I'm Robert."

"Robert wants to buy my company," Ralph says. He's been studying me from the moment I walked into the room.

I narrow an eye, wondering why he finds the need to announce my intentions to the table.

"Media is a long way from architecture," a man sitting three seats left of Ralph says.

Interesting—this fucking stranger knows my background. I loosen my shoulders, sit up straight, and prepare for the worst. I just may have stepped into a trap.

"I would say so," I say.

"Then why buy our company?" says the blonde to my right.

The first thing I wonder is who the fuck she is and why did she say "our" company. Only one owner is named on the prospectus—Ralph Kennedy. I stare at the woman, noticing how her cascading blond hair swallows her narrow face. She's pretty like a mannequin in the window on 5th Avenue, but her eyes are shrewd, and her thin lips are tense. I'd be a fool to pass her off as another pretty face and ignore what I sense, which is an intention to demolish me.

"I'm a businessman." It's the only answer I can muster. Her question is fucking valid. Other than drafting as a hobby, I don't have a lick of real-world experience.

"That's a rudimentary credential, Mr. Tango," she says.

I'm tongue-tied as I study her stern expression. My first inclination is to turn on the charm and endear her to me, but I fight the urge. I've come to the conclusion that I left the bullshitting, flirtatious, and needy part of me back in my old office in New York.

"Well…" Ralph says. "Robert has the ultimate credential."

I rip my eyes off her to look at him.

"I'm waiting to hear it," she says.

So am I.

"He's been recommended by Jack Lord." He sets his elbows on the table and puts his chin on a steeple he's made with his hands. "Highly recommended."

I feel the blonde shrink beside me. Who the hell is she? Ralph's last statement seems to have taken off the pressure. Waiters serve sweet clam-and-tangerine-glaze salads. The conversation turns into a lively discussion about where Ralph should spend his first month of vacation once he officially retires. Normally I'm good at mingling, but at the moment, I'm just too nervous.

However, I find the blonde's self-important attitude interesting. Whenever another guest suggests a destination, the blonde shoots it down. At first I think she's his very young wife. I can see him with a wife more than half his age.

Then a beautiful woman who appears to be in her fifties says, "My husband isn't a fan of such a lovely beach."

Ralph smiles at her appreciatively. "That's true. An ocean should have lines, form, light, and darkness. It should be temperamental and uninviting." He gestures pointedly.

"You're too dramatic, Dad," the blonde says.

Her bold attitude makes sense now. She's a fucking princess who is somehow attached to Ralph's business. I half want to say fuck it and find something else to do with my newfound time and influx of money. As all twenty or so guests continue to kiss Ralph's ass by playing "Where's Waldo" in the form of Ralph's next vacation destination, I consider staying in Napa for a while to renovate my house and develop the land around it. I contemplate the sorts of crops I could plant that are drought resistant. I want to complete the construction on the Roman pool house.

"Where do you think I should go?" Ralph asks.

I've been staring at Ralph but seeing through him, so I know he's talking to me. The table is quiet. I don't feel like playing the "kiss Ralph's ass" game.

"Anywhere the hell you want. It's not a hard decision," I say.

Ralph narrows his eyes as if he can tell that I've gotten impatient. "No, it isn't."

I shrug in agreement.

"You've come into a lot of money recently, yet you've chosen not to take a vacation," Ralph says.

"I would've if the goose hadn't laid the golden egg."

He laughs a little. "And that goose would be me."

I smirk. "The one and only."

Ralph nods then shoots to his feet as he did earlier. "Robert and I have business to discuss. We'll be back."

"But, Dad, we're in the middle of dinner," the blonde says.

Ralph shoots her a look of warning, and I watch her sit back in her seat as if she's just retreated. It's good to see that the old man does have all the power. I wipe my mouth with a cloth napkin and make a vow to myself. If I get up and leave this table, then I'm not coming back. I stand.

"This way," Ralph says.

The suspense in the air couldn't be cut with a chainsaw. I follow Ralph down a dusky hallway with a floor made of black marble and texture-flecked rock walls. The floor and walls create an ambiance that's new to me. Just for that, I take a second and nod once to pay respect to Ralph Kennedy's mastery of creating to evoke feeling.

At the end of the hallway, we take three big block steps down into Ralph's study. A gigantic leather recliner near a wood-burning fireplace sets off the whole room. The rest of the furniture is dark, bulky, and very manly. I can picture Ralph in here in the evenings, smoking a cigar while he drafts plans for the next hotel to hug the shores of France's Blue Coast. The only projects that I'd seen Ralph Kennedy billed as the architect for were European hotel projects. He'd done three projects that I'd seen, and all were for Lord & Lord Development.

Ralph sits in his red recliner. The chair looks as if it were made especially for him. He points at a red leather sofa across from him and alongside the unlit fireplace. "Sit."

I sit, but I don't get too comfortable. "Listen, thank you for seriously considering me as a—"

"So why should I sell to you for any reason other than Jack Lord wants me to?" He sounds as if he's asking me a question I should already know the answer to.

I grunt facetiously. "You can sell your fucking company to whomever the hell you want. That's an interesting table of guests you have out there."

"Indeed."

"How many of them are pursuing your fine company?"

He smirks devilishly. "Five."

"How many have as much money as I have?"

"Zero."

I snort.

"Has Jack given you the financials?" he asks.

"Yes."

"Have you read them?"

"Yes, I have."

"Then you are aware of my dirty little secret?"

I nod. "You're out of money."

"You want my company, Robert, and I want your money."

"Which is the full asking price, regardless of value?"

"That's the only quality that sets you apart from the others."

"Then you have a deal."

He raises a finger. "I need one more thing from you."

I throw up my hands. "What is it?"

"When I started Kennedy Creative, my company was nothing more than an empty building. I was a no-name fresh out of college with a shabby apprenticeship under my belt." He gazes off thoughtfully. "You apprenticed for Barney Arsenault."

"Yes, I did."

"That's a pretty coveted position. How the hell did you not end up in this business?"

That question smacks me like a two-by-four across the face. I'm seeing stars and birds float around my head, and the answer is too shameful to say out loud. I watch him tap the tips of his fingers on the armrest as he waits for my answer.

"I followed the money," I say instead of saying I followed my best friend because I was too afraid to live without him.

He stops tapping his fingers and narrows one eye. "If only I had done it your way. I find money to be power. Don't you?"

"It seems to be the way of the world. But of course, if we valued happiness just as much, it would be power too."

He studies me intriguingly. "Right…" He shifts in his seat. "What do you love the most, Robert?"

The first thing that comes to mind is Vince. I screwed up that relationship with the second thing I love the most, which is pussy. I shift uncomfortably. "I don't know." Not only is my answer a lie, but it's callous.

"When you love something, you want to ensure that it's taken care of."

I'm getting impatient. "Does what you're saying have anything to do with your daughter?"

"Three months," he says.

"Three months for what?"

"I'll give you three months to show me that you can run my operation."

I sniff bitterly. "And what if I say no?"

"You won't. I want to make sure I'm doing the right thing, Robert. You're a former business owner. You should understand my motive."

I take a moment to think about it. He's right. For all he knows, I could come in with my expensive suit, shoes, and bravado and run his business into the ground. "Why three months?"

"I've made some mistakes in running my company. I'm just a damn old dog, and it kills me to learn new tricks."

"Modernism," I say.

He grins as if he's happy to hear me say that. "Right."

"I can give Kennedy Creative that."

"That's what I'm hoping for, and a few more things."

"I'm listening."

"Grace stays on as your VP."

I don't have to be Einstein to figure out who Grace is. "Your daughter?"

He nods.

"That's a big title." Especially for a chick who has already rubbed me the wrong way. I shake my head. "Not as my VP."

Ralph laughs. "I noticed you two didn't get off on the best foot." He shrugs. "Fine, don't keep her as your VP, but keep her on staff."

"Why?"

"I already asked you what you love the most. I love my daughter and my company the most."

Asking me to keep her on board makes no fucking sense to me. "Does she want to stay on board?"

"Very much so."

I shake my head. I don't like this part of the deal. "All right, but we don't put it in the contract. You're just going to have to take my word that I'll keep her on for three months."

"And if she proves valuable to you, then she stays?" He studies the doubt in my expression. "Grace has never received a thing from me without earning it. You'll find her valuable, and that's a promise."

I doubt I will, but I say, "Fair enough. You said a few things?"

"You maintain the company name."

"Ha!" I scoot to the edge of the sofa. I certainly intended to change the company name to RT Creative. "You're asking a lot."

"And so are you. I built that company. I want to be recognized for it."

I want to say, "But you also destroyed it," but I think better of it. I sigh hard and sit back against the sofa. "Fine. Draft up the contract, and I'll have my lawyer look it over."

"The contract is already drafted. I want it signed by morning. And I want you to start by morning."

I open my wallet and take out my lawyer's business card. "Email a copy to the address on the card and my email address on the back."

Ralph takes the card and stands. "Then we have a deal?"

I stand. "Yes, we do."

Ralph extends his hand. We shake on it.

I STARTED USING Jack's lawyer after he helped Vince

and me dissolve that bullshit contract with Peter Oslo. He was Vince's and my original business partner. He fronted the largest chunk of money so that we could start A&Rt Media. The lawyer's name is Richard Darling, and despite the last name, he's a fucking barracuda.

When I called him before I left Ralph's house, I asked him to figure out a way around that company name clause. On my drive back to Napa, I receive a call from him. He's figured out a solution. I call him a genius and ask him to attach my signature to the contract and send it to Kennedy's lawyer.

"There's another clause I want you to be aware of," he says.

"What's that?"

"You said that Kennedy's going to be looking over your shoulder for three months."

"Yes."

"Well, he's not. He's added an asset increase clause."

"What does that entail?"

Darling explains that Ralph Kennedy will be the legal owner for three months, and at the end of three months and one day, ownership will automatically revert to him. The clincher is that the bill of purchase puts the company in an optimal financial state. Ralph needs the contract signed by six tomorrow morning because in three months exactly, he will receive an interest payment in his bank account on assets he has in Kennedy Creative.

"Shit, that's smart of him. Is that fucking legal?"

"It's permissible, but we can get around it. I know you, Rob. You're not Jack Lord. If you like this guy, then don't have me fuck him over, because I can fuck him over. Just say the word."

I look at the lights from Channel Island as I cross the Bay Bridge. I don't want to screw over Ralph even though he's giving me a pretty good fuck-you. But I have to start thinking like Jack and Vince if I want my new business to survive.

"We'll just do what's fair for both of us," I say.

"Got it," Darling says. "I stick to that speed."

"But in three months for sure, I want the name of my company to be RT Creative."

"That's doable."

We leave it at that for now. Once I make it to Napa, Darling has already sent the contract to Ralph's lawyer with changes. I pack a suitcase to stay in the hotel for another week. For the next three months, I'll only spend weekends in Napa. I'll figure out a more permanent living situation at the end of three months.

After I'm packed for the week, I take a few more calls from Darling. By two in the morning, Ralph's and my lawyer have reached an agreement, and I can finally go to bed. The contracts have been signed.

4

IT'S A LEMON

I wake up with pep in my step. I get dressed and hit the road before six. While driving, I receive a text message from Zoe. I quickly read it. I'm to park in the executive lot right off Embarcadero. The message makes me want to tuck my tail and run. *Fuck, this is happening!* There's no turning back.

An hour and fifteen minutes later, I pull up next to a high-end Mercedes Benz with a license plate that says "G. Kennedy." The car is white and flawless. My instincts tell me it belongs to Grace. I check the time on my watch. I'm an hour early, and it kills me that she beat me here. I get out of the car, slam the door, and walk to the office.

The air is cool and moist. The fog is trapped in

the courtyard, and I can barely see through it. I consider slowing my steps, but before my brain can make it happen, something slams into me. I take hold of the body before whoever hit me trips over.

"Oh shit!" a woman says.

Although I keep her from falling, her motorcycle helmet hits the ground. I rush to pick it up, but she beats me to it.

"I got it," she says.

I remember the woman from yesterday. She's prettier up close. There's something familiar about her. Her eyes are light blue. I try to avoid catching a glimpse of her sexy body. She's wearing black jeans and a tight motorcycle jacket. She's hot as hell, but she's one of my employees. I'm turning over a new leaf, trying not to stick my dick in inappropriate places, or pussies.

"Are you okay?" I ask.

"I'm fine," she says, examining her helmet.

"What about that?" I say, nodding at her helmet.

"It's fine." She seems agitated.

I smirk. "I'm sorry. I wasn't paying—"

"Like I said, everything's okay, Mr. Tango." She trots off in the opposite direction.

I watch her until she makes a left and disappears behind the edge of a building. Perhaps my reputation has preceded me, and that's why she got the hell away from me so fast. I'm flooded with shame. I walk, but as I move forward, I make a vow —I'm off women. I'll consider it a pussy diet.

When I make it to my office, Zoe is waiting at the door with a pen and pad. She's bright-eyed and bushy-tailed.

"Good morning, Mr. Tango," she says.

I swear she hasn't stopped smiling since yesterday. "Morning, Zoe," I say, lacking enthusiasm. "You're here early."

She does something between a giggle and a chuckle, and I try not to look annoyed by the sound. "When Ralph told me that you were taking his place this morning, I thought I should get an early start. I figured you would want to be apprised of all the active projects, so I spent the night putting together a detailed project report. If we go to your office, I can explain it all to you." She sets her bright eyes on me.

I'm taken aback by her efficiency. I didn't expect it from her. "Right, and call me Robert."

Her smile gets larger. "Perfect, Robert. I also compiled a list of employees, including their strengths and weaknesses."

I tilt my head. "Did you get any sleep?"

She looks confused.

I smile to let her know I'm joking. "Last night, when you put all the reports together."

"Oh!" She laughs. "No, I didn't compile the employee list last night. It's information that I keep up-to-date, especially when I heard the company was going to be sold. I figured the new owner would want to know his or her employees, right?"

She said that fast. Her tone is annoyingly high-pitched, but each word is concise.

"Well, that's good for your husband," I say.

She frowns. "My husband?"

I look at her ring. "Aren't you married?"

Zoe looks at her hands. "This is my right hand." She said that as though I would have to be a stupid ass to make that sort of mistake.

"Right. Well, let's get to it."

"Okay," she sings and starts toward my office.

I follow Zoe. I'm not the least bit attracted to her. Maybe that's why I can be both repelled by her personality and impressed by her aptitude. Mavis was different. She used to wear this black skirt that was so tight it tucked right under her ass cheeks. Oh, how that skirt made me want to fuck her brains out. I can't picture Zoe naked, which is why it behooves me to let her stick around.

I'm surprised to see Ralph's office is all cleaned out. His framed photos, artwork, and personal trinkets are gone. The black leather sofa and two club chairs have been moved out as well. I'm pretty sure there was a red Aztec-print area rug, and that's gone too.

"Ralph wants you to make the office your own," Zoe says after reading my expression.

I never put personal shit in any of my offices at A&Rt Media. I don't have pictures of family to display, and if I did have them, I'm not sure I'd want to look at the same expressions every day. At least Ralph left the black quartz-top desk and leather office chair. I take his seat. Zoe holds up a finger, gesturing for me to give her a second. She walks out the door and comes back with a metal chair.

She sits. "First order of business: furniture. Do you have a decorative style that you prefer?"

I shrug. "Do you?"

She loses the smile and presses a hand against her chest. "Have a style that I prefer?"

"Yeah," I say easily.

"Are you asking me that because you want me to decorate your office?"

I smirk. "Can you handle it?"

Her eyes grow wide, and the color leaves her face. "Um, sure." She clears her throat. "I mean, yes. Yes…" Her face goes from pale as a ghost to rosy red. You would think I asked her to get naked or something.

"Good," I say. "Now, I'm ready to see that list."

Zoe's looking at my face, but it's as if she's seeing right through me.

"Zoe?" I say.

She snaps out of it. "Sorry."

"No problem. The list?"

"Right. The list…"

"Current projects and personnel list?"

"Oh yes!" She opens the thick, orderly folder she's been clinging to.

The work starts as, one by one, we go through each project. Zoe's knowledge about what's going on around her is impressive. As we go down the list, I get a solid feel for how many architects are assigned to one project, how much it costs, and how long a project takes from conception to completion. I feel my temples pull and my headache grow. Handling the financials for A&Rt Media has helped me get a good idea of what the numbers should look like.

Zoe narrows her eyes at the butt of the pen I'm tapping on the desk. "I see we have a problem."

I lay the pen down. " Perhaps." A name on the list has captured my attention. This person is working on three projects at one time, and the name looks familiar. "Who's this guy, Carter Remington?"

"Carter isn't a guy," Zoe says.

I'm momentarily confused by her response. She's lost the smile, and I think I see her roll her eyes a little.

"From that I gather Carter Remington is a female, but which one?"

Her expression is still stern. "You've seen her. She drives the motorcycle."

I conceal my surprise. I've been around long enough to recognize jealousy among women. I see it in Zoe, and I'm not surprised. Carter Remington is one sexy specimen. Not only that, but I'm sure I've met a girl named Carter who kind of resembles her. The only problem is I can't remember where I met that Carter.

"Is she on the personnel list?" I ask.

Zoe opens her mouth to speak, but whatever she

was about to say is halted by a knock on the glass door. Grace enters without being invited. She's wearing a tight red skirt, and the right amount of cleavage peeks out of her white button-down shirt. She's thin but still shapely. I try to keep my eyes on her face. I do find her physically attractive, and given the right amount of bourbon and whisky, I would probably try to fuck her. At least the old me would've.

"When were you going to come over and talk to me?" Grace asks. She looks as if she has a stick up her ass.

"About what?" I ask.

She throws a cold and dismissive glance at Zoe. "Give us a minute."

Zoe shoots to her feet. "Yes. Okay."

I lift a hand. "Stay seated, Zoe."

Zoe slowly lowers herself back down. I stand so that I can exceed Grace's height. She has good stature for a woman—I estimate that she's 5'10"—but I have a good five inches on her. Grace looks stunned. She's the type of woman who's used to getting her way. I've never had a problem with a woman like that until now.

"Zoe, do you keep my calendar?" I ask.

Zoe's eyes are wide, and her perpetual smile has

faded. I can tell that she's not used to crossing Grace. "Um, yes."

"Then when we're done with our meeting, could you call Grace and schedule a time for her to meet with me today?"

Grace crosses her arms and snorts bitterly. "I'm here to do you a favor, Robert."

"Do me a favor?"

"We're losing clients because my father is —gone."

I shrug nonchalantly. "Let them go."

Grace huffs. "Is that really your attitude?"

I sit back down. My point has been made. "It's not a problem. If a client wants to leave because he's a fan of Ralph's, I can't stop them. That's the nature of fandom."

Grace rolls her eyes then takes a deep breath. She uncrosses her arms. "Robert," she says in a kinder tone, "I have a lunch meeting today, then after that, a meeting with two very worried clients. I would love it if you could delay your meeting with Zoe for at least thirty minutes and lend some time to me."

I crack a smile. Wow, she does have a diplomatic side. It's patronizing as hell but nevertheless more persuasive than the impolite bitch. "Zoe, is it okay if we continue later?"

Zoe looks between Grace and me. "Um, yes."

Grace keeps her glare on me as Zoe walks out the office. Grace is a sore loser of a frivolous war. A woman, or man, who must assert herself in the most meager situation is a sad person. I have a million problems, but that isn't one of them.

Grace takes the abandoned chair. "I would advise you to not fuck your assistant."

She wants to keep fighting until she wins, but I calmly sit back in my chair. "Advice taken. Now what in the hell do you want?"

"I want you to come with me to meet some of our clients."

"Why?"

"Because if you lose them, then I'm sure my father will not sell his company to you."

"The company is already sold to me."

She shakes a finger. "No… you have three months."

"I promised I would keep you on for three months, but I assure you that this company is as good as mine."

Grace frowns as if she's confused. I take a moment to study her expression. What I see is a woman who wanted this operation for herself but feels as though she's been double-crossed. I suspect she ran the company from the day Ralph brought her on board. What baffles me is why her father hasn't told her the whole truth. Our contract is ironclad.

Grace snaps out of it and hands me a sheet of paper. "Here's the list of clients."

I hesitate then take the page and read the names on the list. "I'm familiar with two of the companies."

"All of them are *very* familiar with you," she says.

That sounds like a dig. I ignore her because she can't help herself. Grace is miserable. I was in her shoes about ten years ago, but I sought help.

I spent five years on a shrink's couch, sifting through most of my shit. I stopped going to counseling because I hit a brick wall, and the wall was Vince. The therapist tried to get me to admit the hardest thing to confess—I was jealous of my best friend. I'd hidden the truth deep down inside until Maggie brought it to the surface. She said I fucked her because I wanted to play with Vince's favorite toy. As soon as she said it, the truth swelled up inside me like a hot poison that boiled over. At that moment, I was determined to stop wanting what Vince had, but it was too late. I had already gone past the point of no return.

"If they're so familiar with me, then why in the hell do we need to meet?" I ask.

"So that you can assure them that you're capable."

"I'm not in the business of kissing ass. If they want to go, let them go."

She rolls her eyes and shakes her head. "Are you going to fight me at every turn?"

I look off to ponder. Zoe was pretty intimidated by Grace. I need to let the entire company know with one broad stroke who the fuck is in charge around here. "No. I will have a company-wide meeting tomorrow morning. I would like for you to be there."

She checks her watch. "Well, what time?"

"Nine in the morning."

"That's early."

I show her my classic smirk. "Are you going to fight me at every turn?"

That gets a small chuckle out of her. "Okay, I'll be here." Her skin has turned red. It's nice to know I've still got it.

"Good. See, we're becoming friends," I say.

Grace rolls her eyes and stands. "That remains to be seen." She walks to the doorway then turns. "Since we're becoming friends and all, why don't you come with me tomorrow to meet with Dan Green?"

I shake my finger. "Very good, but the answer is still no—at least for now." I wink.

She narrows an eye curiously. "At least for now?"

"You never know what the future holds."

Grace snorts and walks out of my office. I think she's ascertained that I'm flirting. Instead of calling Zoe back to my office, I head down to the finance department and introduce myself. Each person seems happy that I've taken over, which is good. Richard Hopkins, the chief financial officer, comes out of his office to shake my hand. I ask for the billing statements from the last two years.

"Oh," Richard says as if he's caught off guard by my request. "Well…"

"I need them in the next"—I look at my watch —"I need them now."

He rubs his chin as he thinks. "I guess I can give you access to the database."

I'm smiling Zoe style. "That's perfect."

After receiving access and passwords to all of

the financial databases, I spend hours reading through all of the billing and the architects attached to each project. I compare the details and crunch the numbers. I keep my eyes on the figures, but I notice bodies pass my window all day long. A little after four, Zoe knocks on my door. I look up. She's holding a white bag. I motion for her to come in.

"I bought you naan, four samosas, tandoori chicken, butter chicken, and basmati rice. You do like Indian food, don't you?"

I would joke with her and say no if I weren't so hungry and the figures that I'd studied hadn't revealed some bad news. Basically, buying this company was like buying a lemon.

I pat my pants pocket for my wallet. "Yes, I like Indian. How much do I owe you?"

She holds up a hand. "Nothing. I paid for it with your lunch card."

I don't know what the hell a lunch card is, and Zoe must see the question on my face.

"There's a credit card that I used to buy Ralph's lunch. He was busy all the time too—especially lately."

"Why lately?"

She brings the food to my desk, takes each item out of the bag, and sets it on my desk, careful not to disturb my work. "Ralph has just been stressed out lately. Everybody's been stressed out."

"But not you, right?"

Zoe shrugs. "There." She steps back. "Is there anything else I can get you?"

I wonder why she's being evasive. Maybe she knows what I've just discovered.

"Could you get me that list of employees?" I ask.

"Oh, I left it here." She picks up a folder at the corner of my desk. Her extreme smile has returned, and for some reason, it doesn't irritate me anymore.

I take the folder. "Thanks, Zoe."

"Call me if you need me!" She turns to leave.

"Wait, what's her name again—the one who rides the motorcycle?" I ask.

"Carter?"

"Right. Thanks."

She looks at me as if she wonders why I asked her that, but I don't owe her an answer.

"Another thing—could you send out a company-wide email? I want to have a meeting tomorrow morning at nine."

"Okay," she says. And just like that, she seems to forget how interested she was in why I asked about Carter.

Carter Remington is one of the company's most sought-after architects, but she's been given the most mediocre projects. I've noticed a lot of incomplete project reports where clients decided to pull their account from the company. Carter hasn't had one cancellation, and regardless of how much a client appealed to have her as their architect, she hasn't been put on the project. No wonder she sits in that corner like a shrinking violet. There's definitely been some funny business going on around here, and I plan to end it. Three-quarters of the architects on staff are under the age of thirty and were hired within the last three years. Ralph hired Carter; Grace hired all the others.

I figure out how to buzz Zoe and ask if she can get me all of Carter Remington's, along with four other architects', project packages. She gets them to me in less than fifteen minutes. As soon as I have the packages, I comb through them. What I see is some impeccable work, and Carter's is the best of the bunch.

I look up to rub my tired eyes and notice the clock on the wall. It's seven forty-five at night, yet the office hasn't thinned out. I find that strange. Even Zoe is still at her desk. I buzz her into my office, and she comes right away.

"What can I get you?" she asks.

"Why is everyone still here?"

She looks out the window at the office and shrugs. "I don't know."

"Are they still working?"

"I guess."

The fact that we still have a full house is pretty odd, but my mind is too full to deal with it. I rub my temples. "One more thing—can you get me all of the active project packets?"

"Yes!" It's late, and her eyes are still bright.

"Thanks, Zoe. Once I have the packets, I want you to go home and get some rest. I'll see you in the morning."

"Are you sure? I can stay here as long as you're here."

"No, go. I'll be here all night."

Her eyes grow wide. "All night?"

"All night."

Zoe steps all the way into my office and closes the door. "So can I ask you something?"

I see the worry on her face. "You can ask me anything."

"How bad is it?"

"How bad is what?"

"Are we really in trouble? There have been rumors that there's no equity in this company."

There *is* no equity in this company, but there's potential. I know enough not to disclose any of that to my assistant. I show her my exhausted grin. "Don't worry about anything. I'm on it."

She reads my expression. It takes a while, but what has quickly become one of my favorite smiles returns. "Okay, active projects coming up." She practically skips out of my office.

Once she brings me the active projects, I spend the night combing through them. I haven't been this involved with the business of a company since the early days of A&Rt Media Group, before it got so large.

It's three o'clock in the morning when I look up from the reports and rub my eyes again. I can hardly stay awake. The entire room beyond my office is dark except for one small light in the far corner. If I remember correctly, that's where Carter sits.

I get up and follow the light. The closer I get, the more I'm able to see who's sitting there —it's her.

5

TANGO

S *he* is bent over her desk. Her hand moves across the page like a needle across a polygraph machine. Carter has on earbuds, and I can hear the music coming from them. I'm surprised she hasn't noticed me standing behind her. Judging by the intensity with which her hand is scribbling, she's in the zone. I've been there many times before.

❄

CARTER

"Keep working," Carter told herself.

She felt Robert Tango behind her. His energy

was like a mega wave, washing over her and wiping her out. Who would've thought that he would buy the company she worked for? She wondered if he remembered her. If he remembered her, then he would've hugged her, messed up her hair, and said, "Sup, Carly." He'd always called her Carly instead of Carter. Then he would trot off into the woods with Vince, and they wouldn't return to the main house until just before sundown.

Carter was five years younger than her cousin Vince and his best friend, Robert Tango, but because of the breadth of their personalities and presence, she'd always felt as though they were much older. All of Vince's sisters and cousins had had the biggest crushes on Robert, and she wasn't exempt. He had a natural way of flirting with every person in the room. The first time she'd played with herself, she imagined Robert Tango's sensual and wicked smirk.

She'd seen him mostly during the summers when all of the families vacationed at their great-great-grandfather's estate at Sag Harbor, New York. The house sat on fifteen acres of land adorned with green grass, healthy trees, and muddy lakes. The servants' quarters at the back edge of the property was used as a guesthouse. That was where Vince and Robert stayed. Robert started joining the families on vacation when he was about eleven years old. For the first three years, when Robert and Vince were younger and not yet interested in girls, they spent the summer days swimming in the lakes, climbing trees, catching fireflies, and trying to avoid getting bit by ticks while doing totally gross things like looking for animal carcasses.

Four years later, when the boys turned fifteen, things changed. In one year, they grew taller and filled out. They looked more like twenty-year-old college boys than pubescent teenagers. They were also horny as hell. Vince's sister Allie, who was the same age as Carter, used to accuse Vince and Robert of taking women twice their age back to the guesthouse.

"And do what with them?" Carter asked.

Allie just rolled her eyes and told Carter to grow up. Allie used to talk to Carter as if she knew nothing and Allie knew everything—seventeen years later, that hadn't changed. Allie used her knowledge as leverage. She had always threatened to tell on Vince and Robert if Vince didn't drive her to the movies on his moped or take her shopping for a new swimsuit or something else stupid. Once she made Robert Tango kiss her like he kissed the other girls. He happily obliged, and she never asked again.

Carter knew the kiss had scared Allie. They were taught that good girls waited to have sex with the boy they wanted to marry. Robert Tango had kissed her and dismissed her, and that broke Allie's heart.

That same year, on the day after the Fourth of July celebration, Carter had ridden her bike into town for ice cream. The afternoon was humid but not hot. Her bike rolled to a stop in front of the ice cream shop, and she saw Robert and an older girl inside. The girl giggled about something. He watched her with a sexy smirk. Carter remembered pretending it was her he was watching like that. Then Robert put his hand on the girl's thigh. She looked at her lap and back at him. They shared a moment. Robert whispered something in her ear, and they stood up.

Carter had felt her heart beating and thighs pulsing. They were walking toward the door, so Carter quickly rolled her bike farther down the street so Robert couldn't see her when he walked out of the ice cream shop. Not that he would've recognized her anyway. He only paid her attention on day one, when all the families first arrived. He would mess up her long copper hair and say, "Sup, Carly." Vince would stand behind him grinning, never correcting his friend. Vince laughed and jokingly called her Carly too. Admittedly, she liked the attention. They were the big boys. But she was a little girl, and the big boys only played with big girls.

The girl Robert had left the ice cream shop with was a big girl—not in physical stature but in rank. They got into her white Volkswagen Rabbit. The top was down. Robert put his arm around the girl's seat as she sped off. Carter jumped on her bike and pedaled as fast as she could to follow them. As soon as the car turned down Madison Street, she knew exactly where they were going. Carter over-exerted herself, pedaling as fast as she could back to the estate, except she didn't head to the main house.

Twenty minutes later, she'd reached the guest-house. The white Rabbit was parked in the short driveway. Carter quietly rolled her bike to the side of the house and leaned it against the wall. The window at the front of the house was open. She looked through it, but they weren't in the living room. There wasn't much to the tiny house other than a living room, kitchen, a bathroom, and one bedroom with two twin beds for the boys.

Carter crept around the side of the house. The

bedroom window was open. She heard the girl moaning and Robert grunting. It hadn't taken him long to get between her legs. Carter could only watch him thrust in her for so long. The sight of him enjoying sex with another girl made her sick to her stomach. From that moment on, she had been determined to get over her crush on Robert Tango. After that summer, it was pretty easy. He and Vince turned sixteen and stopped coming up to Sag Harbor for summer vacations. They would go summer skiing in Switzerland, New Zealand, and sometimes Canada.

So it had been so many years since she'd seen her cousin Vince's best friend. She'd almost run into him at Allie's wedding. Rumor had it that he only stayed long enough to watch Allie exchange her vows because weddings made him nervous. Although one drunken night, when Allie came to San Francisco to visit her, Allie confessed that she thought Robert left early because he couldn't bear to see her marry another man.

"And you know this how?" Carter asked.

Allie gave her that same look that used to make her feel like a dork. "I just do."

"Did he say that to you?"

"No, but I know."

For the first time ever, Carter saw right through her know-it-all cousin. Allie's declaration was merely wishful thinking.

Earlier that day, when Carter had slammed into Robert in the courtyard on her way back to her motorcycle to retrieve the new set of drafting pencils she'd bought and left in the storage bin, Carter had thought for sure he would recognize her. He didn't.

As soon as Carter had graduated from high school and entered college, she shedded her over-sized T-shirts and baggy jeans for form-fitting V-neck T-shirts and tight jeans. She dyed her bronze hair black and sliced her long tresses. Her parents had bought her a sensible, fuel-efficient car for college, but Carter got a job as a waitress at a local coffee shop and traded the car in for a motorcycle. A motorcycle had been her primary vehicle ever since.

Carter didn't choose to work late because Robert Tango was in the office. She was pretty sure the crush she'd had on him had fizzled out. She had a client who wanted to change the blueprint mid-construction, and she was figuring out how to alter the structure without losing the integrity. So far, it couldn't be done. Now Robert Tango was standing over her shoulder. She had lost her concentration and was just scribbling anything to make him think she was too busy to be disturbed.

"Still doing it the old way?"

Butterflies fluttered in Carter's stomach. Maybe he'd finally remembered her. She turned to face him. It was as if stage lights illuminated his face. Robert Tango had been a beautiful boy, but wow, he was an even better-looking man.

"The old way?"

He nodded at her hand. "Drafting."

"Oh." She shifted in her seat. "I start by hand drafting then use CAD. It works for me."

Robert lifted his mouth into a dreamy, lopsided smile. "It's pretty late—what are you working on?"

"Um, my clients want me to redraw the plans."

Robert furrowed his eyebrows. "The Sparrow Carter Municipal Library project?"

She nodded.

"What do they want to change?"

Carter's legs and hands were shaking. She tried very hard to control them. "Um, one of their donors wanted to add a last-minute wing in their honor or something."

He grunted thoughtfully. "Can I see?"

"Okay," Carter said off-pitch.

As he strolled over to stand beside her, she noticed that he had loosened his collar. Carter couldn't help but take a deep, slow whiff of him. Robert smelled of curry and sweet soap and shampoo. She had to remember that he still had a reputation of a heartbreaker. Of course, she wasn't the bond-and-breed type. She'd never pictured marriage in her future. Not that she denounced marriage. If a man came along that she wanted to spend forever with, then so be it. Could that man be Robert Tango, the ladies' man extraordinaire, who was probably into far more glamorous women than her? Carter doubted it.

"I see… can I try something?" he asked.

She shrugged, giving him permission to do whatever the hell he wanted.

Carter watched the amazing way he effortlessly traced the pencil across the page and occasionally erased. The rumor was that he had no experience, just a lot of money. Everyone thought he would ruin the company. Half of the architects at Kennedy Creative, including herself, were actively seeking employment elsewhere.

Robert handed the pencil back to her. "There." He gave her that lopsided smile that had always made her stomach drop as if she were riding a rollercoaster.

Short of breath, Carter studied the blueprint. It was amazing. He had removed a series of walls and put them in different places without disturbing the existing structure.

"But how did you even know?" she asked.

"How did I know what part of the structure already exists?"

"Yeah."

He looked at Carter in a way that made her suspect he finally recognized her. "I've been studying the active projects. You're a solid architect, Carter."

The way he looked at her. Carter thought she would burst from desire, so she dropped her face to break eye contact and took a deep breath. "Thank you." She was slightly disappointed that he still had not recognized her.

"You're welcome," he said.

It turned silent. When Carter looked up, Robert was watching her. Carter's heart pulsated just as fast as the nerves in her pussy. For sure he was making her panties wet.

"Well," he said with a sigh, "I guess we should close shop. What do you think?"

"I guess so, since you fixed my dilemma." The way she grinned—she was definitely flirting. So she erased the smile right off her face.

"I'll meet you at the door in five?" he said.

"Five minutes?"

He smirked. "Yes."

Carter gulped. "Okay."

Her entire body tingled as he gave her one last look before walking quickly back to his office. Her breaths were shallow, and her head was dizzy. She thought she would pass out. Robert Tango was her boss. Not in a million years did she think she would ever say those words.

ROBERT

She's flat-out pretty. Carter has a face that makes me think of bushy trees, plush grass, and fireflies. I don't know why I feel that way around her. I shut off my computer, grab my things, turn off the light in my office, and head to our rallying point. Carter's already standing in the doorway wearing her black motorcycle jacket and holding her metallic red helmet. Those objects make for a tough exterior, but the delicate skin of her face and hands are signs of a soft interior.

I shun the desire to picture myself with my face buried in her pussy. Entertaining that fantasy would feel like a huge step backward.

I tap her helmet. "I'll walk you to your motorcycle."

"Okay," she says.

I search the wall for the light switch.

"They're automatic," she says.

I snort. "Thanks."

"You're welcome."

We walk in silence. Carter seems nervous. I hope I haven't crossed any lines. Grace has already said that my reputation precedes me, so I make sure I keep a safe distance between us. The automatic lights cut on as we make our way down the last hallway that leads to the exit. We walk out into the dark morning. The mist is thicker in the courtyard than it was when I arrived to work.

"You have a lot on your mind," I say to break the ice.

Carter looks at me. Her face is young but definitely that of a woman. I would say she's about twenty-five or twenty-six, which is a little young for my tastes. I like a woman who's at least thirty. From that point, the sky's the limit.

"Why have you been reviewing my work?" she asks.

I hesitate. She thinks I'm checking up on her. Maybe that's why she's so anxious. We enter the parking garage.

"I spent the day reviewing everyone's work. I'm trying to figure out each person's strengths and weaknesses."

"Then what are my weaknesses?" she asks.

We walk right past the elevator and up the ramp to the next level.

"You really want to know?" I ask.

"I asked, didn't I?"

"You're heavy on the construction."

She grunts thoughtfully. I watch the wheels turn in her head. We've just walked through the second level, and now we're heading up to the third level. As we round the corner, I see her bike parked right next to the elevator.

"Are you afraid of elevators?" I ask.

She jumps as though I've interrupted her deep in thought. "So Ralph always says, more is more and less is less. Are you saying he's wrong?"

I hesitate. "If he advocates being heavy-handed,

then yes. Don't get me wrong, you do damn good work."

We reach her motorcycle, and she straddles the seat. "Just good?"

I frown to consider the question.

She snorts. "Sorry to make you uncomfortable. Good is good enough."

"Are you a perfectionist?" I ask.

She shakes her head but says, "Yes."

We laugh, but when the laughter simmers down, we're left with awkward silence. I feel good though.

"Have a good night," I say.

"You mean morning," she says.

We smile at each other. Fuck, we're having another moment. I break eye contact by gazing at the rafters.

"I'll see you in the meeting at nine," I say.

Carter kick-starts her bike, and the engine blasts. "Wouldn't miss it," she says over the purring.

She puts on her helmet. I raise a hand to say good-bye. She returns the gesture and zooms off. I watch until she's out of sight.

ONCE I MAKE it back to the hotel, I only have three and a half hours to sleep before I have to head back to the office. I set the alarm on my phone, strip off my clothes, and lie on the bed. My mind is way too active to get any shut-eye. It's jammed with thoughts of Grace, Zoe, the financial reports, and my plan to avoid a common disaster. From what I've gathered, the company has been losing clients because the quality of work has suffered because projects have been divvied out unfairly and not according to architects' strengths. I feel Grace has something to do with the shabby way the company has been run. Ralph has been letting her get away with bloody murder. Why do I feel so uncomfortable about what I have to do at this morning's meeting? I'm not sure how my changes will be received. I've learned that people hate change, but Kennedy Creative is my stallion to ride. Everybody needs to know it'll be run the way I see fit.

MY CELL PHONE ALARM CHIMES. I sit up and rub my eyes. I didn't even realize I had fallen into a deep sleep. My head's woozy. I could use a fifteen-minute snooze, but there's no time. I put on a pair of jeans and a crisp shirt. Yesterday I was the only person in the office wearing a suit. I like the current laid-back culture, and I want to become acclimated to it. Room service knocks on the door to bring my breakfast. I like that they're prompt.

Exhaustion bears down upon me, but I allow my motivation to energize me. I scarf down the eggs, bacon, hash browns, and toast. I drink the entire carafe of coffee and head out. I take the lack of heavy traffic as a sign that this morning's meeting will be productive. I make it to the complex, park, and hurry into the building. It looks as though everyone is here, and the tension is thick. I say good morning to inquisitive faces as I walk down the aisle to my office. Pinched by curiosity, I turn toward Carter's desk. The light is out, and she isn't in yet.

"Robert," Zoe sings.

I look to the left, and she's right beside me as if she came out of nowhere. "Morning, Zoe."

"Do you need help prepping for the meeting?"

"Yes, please," I say.

"Do you need breakfast?"

"No."

"Coffee?"

"No. Just your smiling face." I can't believe I said that.

She blushes, and one of the female workers who heard what I just said widens her eyes. That reputation of mine is like the plague. I fight the urge to hide inside my own skin and beat myself up for putting myself in a position where I look like a cad.

"Go to your desk. I'll send you an email. I want you to print some information before the meeting starts," I say.

"I'll be waiting," Zoe says and scurries away.

I think she's still blushing. The days when I could be flippant about my interactions with the opposite sex are over. I have to watch myself, or I could be facing a sexual harassment suit.

I get to my desk and email Zoe a list of thirty-three vendors. I need her to make sure the outstanding balances owed to each are paid from an account I'll have finance set up by the end of the day. I let her know that no requests are to be sent to the vendors until contracts are renegotiated. I also have her contact a headhunter I know in New York. It's time to restructure the departments, hire some new department heads, and make this company run like a well-oiled machine. My reign at Kennedy Creative has officially started.

6

THE GIRL WITH THE RED METALLIC MOTORCYCLE HELMET

*G*rumbling erupts in the conference room. I've just laid out my immediate plan for change, which includes switching architects for just about every active project. I've created teams with the five best architects as the new senior architects who will oversee the projects assigned to them. There's been too much autonomy, which is why spending has gone through the roof.

"Glad to get that out of the way," I say, referring to the complaining.

I've learned from Vince that when there's hostility in the room, the person in charge should never open the floor up for questions. He controls the reins from beginning to end.

"Warren, David, Rose, Justin, and Carly, meet me in my office directly after this meeting," I say.

Zoe, who's sitting in the front, makes a noise to get my attention. "You mean Carter."

I whip my gaze to Carter's face. "Right. And Carter."

Carter breaks eye contact to stare into her lap. A face from the past comes to mind. That girl had longer and lighter hair. They bear some resemblance to each other, but it has been almost two decades since I've seen Vince's cousin Carter. They can't be one and the same. Could they? My peripheral vision catches a hand that goes up in the air. I had lost my train of thought, but I quickly find it.

"If you have any questions, shoot me an email, and I'll try to address your concerns."

Grace chuckles bitterly. She had been sitting so quietly that I forgot she was in the room. I expected her to give me flak from the moment I opened my mouth.

"You can't fire a machine gun and not receive return fire," she says.

The suspense is thick in the air. I don't practice referring to a woman as a bitch, but in this case, it would be true.

"Actually, I can," I say specifically to Grace,

then I address the varied expressions in the room. "As I said, if you have something to say, then email me. If I don't respond, then you can at least know that you've been heard. I'm investing my time and my capital in this company. Last month, there were eight layoffs. A few of your best colleagues were let go. I'm going to pursue the talent we lost, but I'm also going to make sure that we are solid. You leave how that's going to occur to me. All I need is for each of you to do your best work, from operations all the way to design staff. My plan will work, people. Kennedy Creative will be back on top in no time. If you want to be part of the rise, then it's your decision, but you make that choice today. Tomorrow, you'll be working in your teams, and each team will be assigned specific support staff."

I gauge their reactions. No one appears more pissed off than Grace. I end the meeting, and all systems are a go. I start by meeting with the five principal architects. I avoid looking for signs of Carly in Carter. Instead, I ask them all if they're on board and ready for the hard work to come. I'm glad to hear that they're all in.

For the first week, I pull late nights and early mornings, bringing structure to the company. I reform the residential and corporate departments and create a new industrial department. I interview possible new hires for my management team. I'm in nonstop meetings with the most difficult clients who are resistant to change. By week two, Jack Lord agrees to meet with me. I use his in-depth knowledge of residential and corporate development to strengthen our vendors list so that we can get quality products at the best price.

"It looks different around here," Jack says as he examines the hustle and bustle beyond my office windows.

"By the way you're grinning, I would say that's a good thing," I say.

Jack laughs. "I knew you could pull this fucking place out of the ashes."

I want to ask Jack how in the hell he knew that. I've been the fuck-up owner of A&Rt Media for as long as I could remember. Instead I say, "Thanks for your confidence in me." I sigh and lean back against the backrest of my chair. "I have to say, this is exactly what I needed."

I catch a glimpse of Carter walking past my office. I've tried to ignore her for the last two weeks. This morning, she arrived without her motorcycle helmet. She's had lunch with Matt Franks, one of the architects on her team, three times this week. I've tried to not let their association bother me, but I can't help it. I'm attracted to her. But she's my subordinate, so there's nothing I can do about it. I've resisted the desire to call Vince and ask about his cousin Carter. If she is *the* Carter that I couldn't stop calling Carly, then I don't know what the hell I'll do. However, I'm not ready to reach out to Vince, not yet.

"Anyway, how's A&Rt post RT?" I ask.

Jack tosses his head back and laughs. "The same as it was during RT."

I snicker. "Right."

He fills me in on his wife, Daisy's, pregnancy. She's not well. Then he mentions that Maggie has been living in his house in Malibu.

"With Vince?" I ask.

"They've broken up," Jack says.

That revelation hits me like a two-by-four upside the head. I want to shrink in my seat. I know I'm the reason they're apart. I'm resolved on my decision to win back Vince's friendship. The next time I see Vince, I want him to believe that he can trust me. The steady diet of no pussy, no marijuana, and no whiskey or cigarettes has done me good. If all I had to do was work like a fire ant, then I could've kept my libido under wraps long before now.

Jack and I say good-bye, and I get back to work. Zoe does a good job of keeping my calendar updated. The only hours that I have free are for lunch. When I consult my calendar, I see that I have a meeting with Carter and a client from Bounty Mountain Resort in ten minutes.

I push the butt of my pen up and down as I think. It wouldn't take long for me to make a quick call to Allie and ask what Carly, I mean Carter, is up to these days. I make a split-second decision, take out my cell phone, and call her.

"Robert?" Allie says.

"Hey, Allie," I say.

"What the hell have you done?"

I'm taken aback by her tone. I also realize that she's not going to let me keep the call short and sweet. "Hey, your cousin Carter, what is she doing these days?"

"Huh?"

"That's all I wanted to ask you."

Zoe knocks on the window and points at her watch. I shout a string of curse words in my head.

"What's going on with you and Vince?" Allie asks.

Vince always keeps personal business away from his sisters. They're nosy as hell and equally judgmental. They never liked Maggie because she's not the kind of woman they pictured him with. That's why they practically shoved their friend Emily Callahan, who's perhaps the most boring woman on the planet, on top of his dick, hoping she had what it took to make him forget about Maggie.

I sigh out of frustration. "Shit, Allie, I have to go. Call me back and leave a message."

"A message about what?"

"Your cousin Carly."

"Carter."

Zoe knocks on the window and points at the clients, who are walking into the conference room.

I shoot to my feet. "Allie, just call me back and leave a message."

"She's in San Francisco," she says in a rush.

I fall back into my seat and massage my temples. "She wouldn't happen to be an architect, would she?"

"Yes, she's an architect. I think… yes, she is."

"Did she cut and color her hair?"

Allie snorts, and I can picture her rolling her eyes. "She went through a rebellious phase. I think she's over it. I'm not sure. Lexie had lunch with her in San Francisco last month, and she said Carter's still riding that motorcycle. Why do you ask?"

I feel as if the wind has been knocked out of me. "No reason."

"Don't give me that shit, Tango. Are you screwing with her?"

"I got to go," I say.

"Tango—"

I hang up.

Now that I can no longer delude myself, I allow myself to see the resemblance between the Carter of today and the Carly of yesteryear. Fuck, she *is* Vince's younger cousin. I look at Zoe, and she's staring at me. Her face has turned red. I show her the thumbs-up and slowly rise from my seat. When I walk out the office, Zoe pushes the meeting packet into my hands and follows me to take notes. Behind that smile of hers is a shitload of anal-retentive traits; one of them is being on time for meetings. Last Wednesday, she had a panic attack at a stop-light because we were five minutes late for an off-site meeting.

The door to the conference room is open. I step aside to let Zoe pass, and Carter and I lock eyes. She looks more tired than usual. Like the other principal architects, she's been working around the clock. However, I now understand why she looks at me the way she does. She has been waiting for me to recognize her.

I shake the clients' hands. "Nice to meet you, April and Celia." The two women are building a yoga and spa retreat in the Santa Barbara hills.

April and Celia shoot each other a look as they shake my hand.

"Wow, you're handsome," Celia says.

April gives me a smoldering look. "Very handsome."

Carter rolls her eyes.

CARTER

Carter knew her clients, April and Celia, would make eyes at Robert Tango. Every woman in the office had a crush on him. Carter had tried to downplay the fact that he was gorgeous, sexy, and competent, which made him even sexier. In a matter of two weeks, he had changed everyone's opinion of him. The chicks wanted to marry him, and the guys wanted to be his disciples. But Carter had a sneaking suspicion that Robert Tango had no idea he was quickly becoming a demigod for pulling Kennedy Creative out of the ashes.

Robert grinned at the clients and Carter. "So I'm sure Carter has been a great benefit to you." He took a seat beside her.

"We're not sure Carter shares our vision," April said.

Carter wanted to scowl at her, not because April had thrown her under the bus but because she didn't forget to bat her eyelashes at Robert in the process.

He opened the meeting packet and carefully scanned each page. "Carter has drafted six different blueprints for you. You initially went with plan number 3645, but three months later, you asked to make adjustments."

"Right," April said with a bite.

Carter avoided the desire to roll her eyes. Ever since she started working with April and Celia, they'd been a problem. They didn't respect her knowledge and had been trying to figure out how to be assigned a new architect without outright asking for a man to handle their project. Carter saw them as the kind of women who felt feminine power was in the figure, face, and pussy, not the mind.

"These plans are solid, but I understand that

you want to build a healing pool where the foundation has already been poured and the structure framed," Robert said. "Did Carter explain that the contractors had difficulty with the foundation and what had to be done to stabilize it?"

"Yes, but it's not hard to tear it all down and put a hole in the ground."

Robert spread the plans on the table. "Actually, what you're asking the builders to do is pretty difficult and very expensive."

"I understand, but without the natural pools, our resort will be like any other hippie, orgy, bird-food destination that's stuck in the woods," Celia said.

Robert chuckled, and Carter cringed. Strangely, the fact that Celia could make him laugh made Carter jealous. The emotion alarmed Carter. She had convinced herself that she had gotten rid of the schoolgirl crush she'd had on him.

"By the way, when the resort is up and running, you have lifetime access," Celia said now that she had him on her hook.

Robert looked at Carter with a hint of a smile, then he winked at Celia. "Thanks for the offer."

Carter knew it was time to say something in her own defense, but her head was floating from the look he had just given her. "I tried to present another blueprint, but"—she threw up her hands —"they didn't want to see it."

"We thought six was enough," April said snobbishly.

Carter felt like accusing April and Celia of making her job hard because not only was she a woman, Carter was an attractive woman. If she looked like Beavis, then they would have been kissing the ground she walked on. Her team had done superior work for them. Construction had had no problems implementing the plans. Appliance and fixture deliveries had been on time and installed without difficulty. The clients had purposely thrown challenges at Carter from the beginning, and she had answered every one of them.

"Do you have it?" Robert asked Carter.

"We don't need another blueprint," April said. "Just tear the fucking thing down and put in the healing pool."

"It's right here," Carter said.

Robert grimaced at Carter's shaking hands when she handed him the blueprint.

Celia looked at April with panic. "We were thinking we needed fresh eyes."

"Did you know that Carter is one of our best, if not the best architect, we have on staff?" Robert looked up from the drawing. His gaze shifted between the two clients.

"Well, that's great but—" April said.

"But she hasn't made one mistake on this project. She's given you everything you've asked for until you requested the outlandish. But even then, she figured out a creative and inexpensive way to give you what you asked for."

He handed the blueprint to Celia, and Carter took an inward sigh of relief. Ralph would've never stood up for her like that. Ralph believed in giving the client what they wanted no matter what. He would've assigned a man to their account, and that guy would've presented Carter's work to Celia and April. Then they would've dubbed him a genius. *The bitches*.

Celia reluctantly scanned the blueprint. "I don't understand this."

"Well, then, we'll help you," Robert said.

He called them all to the table and asked Carter to explain the addition, which she gladly did. Thirty minutes later, the clients had accepted Carter's fix and agreed to pay for it. Robert also made them agree to make no more changes. On the way out,

April and Celia shook Robert's hand, flipped their hair, and grinned like crushing schoolgirls. It was clear that they weren't going to say good-bye to Carter, so she gathered her meeting materials and headed for the door behind Zoe.

"Carter, could you stay for a few minutes?" Robert asked.

She turned around. April and Celia were giving her that repellent gaze that she was used to receiving from them. The expression said, "I wish I never had to see you again."

"Sure," Carter said and sat in the nearest chair. She opened her folder and pretended to study the blueprint on top.

"So, Robert, are you single?" April asked.

He tossed his head back and chuckled. "I don't date clients."

"Well, how about you take me to dinner to discuss the healing pool?"

Carter caught the glance Robert shot her. She wondered what it meant. Maybe he was nervous and thought it was her job to keep her client on a leash.

Carter raised her hand. "Listen, I'll sit down with you any time to talk healing pools. I've helped clients choose and install them before."

April gave Carter that same expression.

Robert smiled. "Well, there you have it." He put his hand on Celia's back and guided them to the door. "Thank you so much for making the trip to meet with us. Zoe?"

Zoe was still standing outside the door. "This way, ladies," she said with a mega smile.

April and Celia gazed at Robert as they followed Zoe. As soon as they were all of the way out of the room, Robert closed the door. Carter gulped, and anxiety seized her. She saw him walking as if he were moving in slow motion. He sat beside her and looked her right in the eyes.

Robert

I HAVEN'T a clue of what to say. Carter is no longer the quiet little girl who studied everything around her. She's a fully formed woman, and oddly enough, I want to get to know her.

"Thank you for sticking up for me," she says, watching me with wide eyes.

She looks so vulnerable. I want to kiss her. "It was a no-brainer, although I'm going to call the contractors and ask if they can get it done in the next three days. I want those chicks out of your hair. They got the best architect for the lowest price. That won't happen again."

They were jealous of Carter, that was for sure. She's hotter and smarter. I've said no to those loopy hippie chicks all my life. They think they're different from women like Vince's sisters and Emily Callahan, but other than their grimy unwashed yoga wear and see-through shirts with no bra, they're pretty much cut from the same cloth.

Carter raised an eyebrow. "So you really meant that B.S. about me being the best architect on staff?"

"Hell yeah!" I say, grinning Zoe style.

"What about Brent?"

"He's good, but you're better."

Carter studies me as if she's trying to gauge whether or not I'm being truthful. The fact that I'm picturing her naked on top of the conference room table with my face between her legs makes me question my own sincerity. I look away from her face to banish the salacious thought.

"Well, thanks," she says.

"You're welcome. Hey, do you have lunch plans?" I ask.

She tilts her head. "No. Why?"

"I was thinking we could, you know, have lunch and talk."

"Talk about what?" she says nervously.

"I want to talk about today and your future with this company." I didn't pull those topics out of my ass. Before learning Carter's true identity, I had planned to sit down with her to discuss future projects.

"Well, okay then," Carter says.

I'm relieved. "Okay then."

I DRIVE, and Carter rides shotgun. There are a lot of cars on the road during the lunch hour, but I plan to drive into the city and try a restaurant there. My passenger has been quiet, but she's been rubbing her fingers together nonstop. She's nervous. Probably because she still thinks I don't remember her.

"So," I say. "You've changed your hair, and you're all grown up."

I'm stopped behind a parade of cars. I turn to face her opened-mouth gaze.

"You remember?" she asks.

"I spoke to Allie."

She turns her whole body in my direction. "When?"

"Before the meeting."

She sighs as if she's finally releasing the tension in her body. As we roll along, we talk about summer vacations in East Hampton. Carter and I laugh about how Vince and I used to pick up college girls when we were fifteen.

"I didn't think you were paying attention," I say.

Carter drops her face bashfully. "I was paying attention." Her face has turned red, and she's fiddling with her fingers again.

"Oh yeah?" I'm intrigued.

"I, um, I..."

I slam on my brakes to avoid running a light and shoot one arm out across the passenger seat to make sure Carter doesn't slam into the window.

"Sorry about that," I say as I check the car behind me. Good thing he maintained some distance. "You were saying?"

"Nothing, um, where are you going?"

"Downtown. There's a restaurant across from my hotel."

"It's going to be hell trying to make it downtown. Why don't we just go to Yao Fun?" she asks.

"Nice name. Where is it?"

"It's in the Richmond neighborhood on Balboa. It's only about fifteen blocks that way." She points west.

"How can I turn down Yao Fun?" I say, sort of mocking the name.

She laughs, and I make a sharp right onto Balboa. Carter seems more comfortable in my presence now, and I like it, a lot. I get lucky and find a parking spot in front of the corner restaurant. The restaurant is so small that if you blink, you'll miss it. Before we walk in, a small man opens the door and speaks to Carter in Chinese. She replies in Chinese. I raise my eyebrows, surprised and impressed.

We're seated near the window and given menus. It's all written in Chinese.

"Just tell me what you like, and I'll order it for you," she says.

I crack a smile. "Are you going to give me a reading?"

"I could, but I'm sure you've eaten at plenty of Chinese restaurants."

I shrug. "Sure, I have."

She leans against the wall with a cool kind of manner and picks up her chopsticks. "They have everything here. Mr. Ping will make anything you ask for. He's like the Genie."

It's so hard to believe that this sexy, deep woman is the same girl whose name I could never remember. I would've never thought Vince's cousin would turn out to be the person seated across from me.

"Right. Although it would be kind of fun to have you give me a reading. It'll be like a poetry reading." I flex my eyebrows.

Carter picks up the menu and reads it in Chinese. "And now the interpretation," she says playfully. She reads the same block in English.

"And you continue to impress me," I say. "So how did you learn Chinese?"

"When I was in high school, my father suggested that I learn two languages—Mandarin and Spanish. My dad was always pretty smart, so I followed his advice."

"Goodness, I'm so damn impressed by you."

She looks at me like a deer trapped in head-lights. I'm worried that I've overstepped my boundaries. I have enough experience with women to know that a few more good lines, smirks, and the right kind of eye contact would land her in my bed. I want her, but that doesn't mean a goddamn thing. I wanted every single woman I fucked and forgot. I'm not convinced that I wouldn't do to Carter the same thing that I did to all the rest, so I take the twinkle out of my eyes and sit back in my seat.

The waiter comes to take our order.

"Ladies first," I say.

She orders in Chinese. She tells me she ordered two tea services. "Water?"

I nod. "Sure." I see that she has a modest demeanor, but deep down, she likes to be in control. "And I'll have the Peking duck with rice noodles sprinkled with sesame oil and ginger."

She smirks as if she's impressed then relays my order. They go back and forth. The waiter looks at me as if I made the mistake of diverting from the vast list of items that they serve. Carter says something else.

The waiter says, "Okay."

"Okay," she says.

He takes our menus.

"Did I just see a battle?" I ask.

She laughs and measures with her thumb and forefinger. "A small one."

I'm pretty aware that I'm staring. Her face has such pretty bone structure, and her eyes are pure blue. I snap out of it. "So you're from Denver, right?"

"No. My cousins are from Denver. I grew up in Pasadena."

I'm taken aback. "Your family used to travel to Sag Harbor all the way from Pasadena every summer?"

Carter grunts cynically. "I used to ask that same question every year, at least until you showed up." She quickly looks away as if she's said too much.

I'm not sure how I should respond. The damn complications are in the way. "Sag Harbor was a sweet getaway."

She smiles and nods, although I can see the turning thoughts behind her eyes.

"What are you thinking?" I ask.

"I'm thinking that you never noticed me back then, and that's why you needed Allie to enlighten you today." She sounds disappointed.

"I noticed you." I'm not lying—I did notice her.

She snickers. "Yeah, you would mess up my hair and call me by the wrong name."

"I thought you were cute—young but cute."

"You're not that much older than I am."

We turn toward the waiter, who arrives with the food. Carter has ordered a feast. One by one, he puts down the dishes. I count them as they hit the table. Carter reads my expression and chuckles.

"Is this a joke?" I ask.

She shakes her head. "No. I'm starving, aren't you?"

I grin like I never have. I can't figure Carter out, but I like how she just made me feel. "I am now."

Carter flexes her eyebrows and pulls her chopsticks apart. "Then dig in."

I pull apart my chopsticks. I follow Carter's lead and eat from whichever plate I choose.

"As your boss, I'm not allowed to ask your age, but if you want to share that information, then I'm ready to hear it."

Carter puts a helping of sautéed seaweed into her mouth. She narrows her eyes as she chews and swallows. "I don't want to tell you."

I flinch. "Why not?"

"Because you're an ageist."

"What?" I ask, intrigued.

"You always liked older women. I see you looking at Grace's ass. She's thirty-five, just so you know."

I'm trying to remember a time when I focused on Grace's barely existent ass. "You're seeing things. I've never noticed Grace's ass."

Carter shrugs. "Anyway, how old do you think I am?"

I study her pretty face. "Twenty-five."

She grunts.

"I'm right, aren't I?"

"Probably. Probably not."

"Hey, there's nothing wrong with being twenty-five," I say to make her feel better about revealing her age.

She shrugs.

"Young and fluent in Chinese and Spanish? I say that you're the one who's winning." I smile.

"Me? You're the one who's phenomenal. Look at you. You're a billionaire! I knew that one day you were going to be something."

There I go grinning again. I fight the urge to downplay my role in A&Rt Media's success. I would've been comfortable doing it, but I recently realized that I'm the one who stayed on top of our finances. I read the books and asked Gabe to make the appropriate changes. I might have been deficient in the media aspect of the business, but in the financial growth aspect, I was spot on.

"Wow. Thanks," I say.

She shrugs. "So about the real reason why we're here."

I realize that was a question. The real reason is that I wanted to spend some time out of the office with her. "Yes. Work."

"Of course work. Robert Tango didn't want to play with me then; why would he play with me now?" she says with a smile.

A multitude of images of Carter and I playing with each other now shuffle through my thoughts. Suddenly, I realize that I've been staring at her for far too long. My mouth is watering, and my dick is firm.

I tilt my head inquisitively. "Did you have a crush on me back then?"

Her face turns red, and she helps herself to a serving of what looks and smells like ginger shrimp. "Did you know I had a crush on you?"

"No, I didn't."

She takes a deep breath. "Okay, I'm going to tell you this story because it weighs on me whenever your name is spoken."

I try to focus on what she's saying as she recalls a memory of me and a girl I met at the ice cream shop. I took her back to the "love shack," which was the guesthouse at the back end of Vince's family's summer estate. She says the girl drove me back to the guesthouse in a Volkswagen and that I fucked her.

"I was looking through the window." She rolls her eyes in shame. "Like a peeping Tammy."

I laugh. "A peeping Tammy?"

"The female version of Peeping Tom."

"So you're apologizing for watching me fuck some girl? How long did it take for me to make it to the end?" I wink at her.

"You can't remember?"

"I remember fucking like a fifteen-year-old kid. I never lasted that long."

She stares at me as if a lot of thoughts are floating through her head. She chuckles. "Well, you didn't."

"Last that long?"

"Right."

I've never laughed this hard in my life.

She shrugs squeamishly. "Oh, and I'm sorry for peeping."

"Apology not necessary. I brought a boatload of girls back to the house and fucked them." I wish I could say that I'd done it because I was young and stupid, but I haven't really shed that behavior. I imagine that if the opportunity to purchase a failing architecture firm hadn't presented itself, then I would be philandering through Europe, fucking, drinking, and getting high until I suffered a heart attack and died. Basically, I would be in the final stretch of the path to self-destruction. "Not saying it was right, but I did it."

She looks at me with narrowed eyes. "Are you judging yourself, Robert Tango?"

I sit back. What a hefty question. "Yes, I am, and it's about time."

"That never solves anything, you know," she says.

"No?"

"You can't go back and change the past. Plus no one should judge anyone, and we sure as hell shouldn't judge ourselves."

"Oh no? So what do you recommend?" I ask.

"Self-reflection and revision."

I chuckle. She's quick. I like that. "When did you become what you are?" Shit, I wish I could take that back.

Carter's face turns red again. I've embarrassed her. We smile at each other and allow the awkward moment to pass.

"Regarding work…" I say.

We laugh.

"I want to use your talents on our key projects."

She starts eating again. "Define key projects?"

I nod, impressed by her question. "There are a handful of clients who will keep us afloat no matter what. I've read their completed project reports. There's a sixty-five percent satisfactory rate."

She stops before putting a helping of one of the chicken dishes into her mouth. "Wow, that low? Was I an architect on any of the projects?"

"Not one of them."

"That's a relief." She plops the food into her mouth.

I watch her lips as she chews, then I blink myself back to the moment. "But if you were the architect for all the projects, then the clients would've been satisfied. Not only are you a talented drafter, but you're a thorough project manager."

"That's because I don't have a social life." Carter chuckles.

"A woman who rides a motorcycle has no social life? Sounds like an oxymoron."

"Most contradictions are not contradictions."

"I beg to differ," I say.

She tilts her head in a challenging way.

"Hot contradicts cold. Night contradicts day. Good contradicts evil. And in all of those cases, the line that sets the two apart is clear and concise."

Her eyes shine as she grins. "Then I stand corrected."

Our gazes linger on each other. I had no idea she would have this sort of effect on me. It's different and surprising. In order to excise the sexual chemistry brewing between us, I pick up the conversation about work and where I see her talents being used in current and future projects. Carter listens attentively and asks all the right questions. We eat and talk, and occasionally fall into lingering stares. Fuck, I'm falling for this woman, who just happens to be Vince's cousin, and I don't want to stop.

On the way back to the office, I ask Carter how she used to spend her days in Sag Harbor when we all were there. I only remember seeing her at the breakfast table, because Vince and I learned that if we made it to breakfast each morning, then his mother wouldn't question what we did the night before or what we had planned for the day. We were fifteen years old and most of the time drunk as hell, but nobody but Vince's sisters, Allie and Madison, could tell.

"I mostly rode around on my bike looking at everything."

"Everything? Like what?"

"I went out in search of construction sites mostly. I've always been fascinated by the ground-up process of an edifice. I would walk through the bare bones of a house and try to figure out where all the rooms should go." She smiles reflectively. "I know it sounds nerdish, but it's the truth."

"That doesn't sound nerdish. I wish you had told me. I would've gone with you."

She laughs. "Oh, is that so?"

I grin at her as I pull into the executive's parking stall. "In hindsight, I would've."

The warm smile we share seems so natural.

"I still do it," she says.

We haven't broken eye contact.

"Do what?"

"On the weekends, I look for new construction and roam the grounds."

"You do?"

She nods. "Yeah, I do."

"I'd like to go with you sometime. Do you mind?"

Carter's smile fades. "Um, no, I don't mind."

There's a knock on my window, and Carter and I look to see who's there. Grace steps back and folds her arms in front of her. I'm already dreading interacting with her. Two more months, then she's out of my hair.

Carter gets out of the car before I can turn toward her. When I open my door to get out, Carter's already walking down the ramp. I'm still baffled about why she doesn't use the elevator or stairs.

"I've been looking for you. Zoe said you went to lunch two hours ago."

I shake the confusion out of my head. "Sorry, but when did I start needing to check in with you?"

"You don't, but you're running a business here, and not so you can fraternize with the help."

"What the fuck do you want, Grace?" I'm this close to reneging on my word and putting her ass out of my company now.

She grunts huffily. "I need you to accompany me tonight."

"Accompany you where?"

"To an event."

I tilt my head. "Give me a straight answer. What the hell do you do around here?"

"I've done everything."

I slam my door. "Is there a job title for *everything*?" I stomp toward the elevator, and I hear her heels clicking behind me. "Well, if you're going to work in my company, then we're going to find you a job title, and you're going to stick to it."

I'm being rude as hell, but Grace brings out the jerk in me.

She jumps ahead of me and puts her hand over the down button. "How dare you?"

The door opens, and two people exit. I enter the elevator. Grace enters too since she's not finished gabbing.

"And why are you having dinners and shit in the first place?" I ask.

"Why are you going to lunch with Carter?"

"It's none of your business. You didn't answer my question."

"Or did you even go to lunch? Did you take her to your hotel room and fuck her?"

My frown is so severe that I feel as if my face will cave in. "What do you want, Grace?" I enunciate each word.

"I said that I want you to go to an event with me."

"What's the event?"

"The Annual Soiree at City Hall," she says.

"Why do I need to be there?"

"Because everyone we need to work with to get shit done in this city will be there."

I ruffle my eyebrows. The elevator door opens, and I get out.

Grace stays in and puts her hand in the doorway. "Meet me in the lobby of that hotel you're staying in at eight thirty tonight. Don't be late. Wear a black suit with a black tie. I would say not a cheap suit, but you haven't worn anything inexpensive since you waltzed into my father's office asking to buy his company." She takes her hand out of the doorway. "Tonight, you're going to see what I do." Her tone is bitter. Apparently, she's not only offended me, but I've offended her as well.

I make it back to the office, and Carter is at her desk, working. She doesn't look in my direction as I pass her door and head to my office. I feel as if I'm caught in the calm before a storm. I push down the giddy sensation I get in my stomach when I remember today's lunch, and I get to work.

I meet with Account Acquisitions and listen to each project they want to place a bid for. They tell me about the solicitations from private individuals, non-profits, and businesses who want to use our services. The majority of the solicitations are from non-profits. Ralph was big on signing onto free projects, but I'm not. I end that meeting three hours later and start another one.

The office starts to thin out around six, but I've been so busy that I forgot to look in on Carter. When I finally look toward her desk, it's clean and she's gone. I look at the other side of the room where Matt sits. He's gone too. Shit, I'm jealous, and not in the way I've been toward Vince. This is different. This is something that I can't explain.

7

PRINCIPALS

I take the elevator down to the hotel lobby. Grace is already there, sitting on one of the sofas and looking at her cell phone. She's wearing another tight bright red dress. Some guy almost trips over his own feet while staring at her. She's certainly beautiful, and I'm normally drawn to bitches, but for some reason, she doesn't do it for me. If I hadn't been drawn to Carter upon first glance, I wonder if I would be boning Grace right now. The thought makes my stomach turn.

Grace stands once I reach her. "You're on time."

"I've been punctual ever since I took over the helm."

"Well..." She straightens my collar, and I fight

the urge to recoil. "I heard punctuality wasn't your style."

I guide her hands away from my collar. "And who told you that?"

"Does it matter?"

I shrug. "No."

She snorts facetiously. "I didn't think so. The limo is waiting for us." She holds out her elbow. "Be a gentleman."

I take her arm, and we walk side by side out of the lobby and to the limo. I sit as far away from her as possible. Grace starts sending texts as soon as the car moves. It's a relief to not have to chitchat with her.

"So what's going on between you and Carter?"

I'm caught off guard. "Didn't you ask that already?"

"And you didn't answer."

"Because it's none of your business."

She finally looks up from her phone. "You should watch out for her. She likes—attention."

I recall the funny, sexy, down-to-earth young woman, who spends her weekends hunting for construction sites, that I had lunch with today. There's no way Carter is the kind of woman who needs to be seen. "Duly noted."

She slips her phone inside of her purse. "Is that so?"

"Is your problem with her or me?"

"Who says I have a problem?"

I grunt. "Listen, I took my best architect to lunch to discuss the sorts of projects she'll be working on in the future."

"Ha! Carter is not your best architect."

"And you determined this how?"

She rolls her eyes and looks out the window.

I study her for a moment. "You're jealous of her. Why? She's an architect, and you're daddy's little girl. You're both attractive in your own ways. Believe me, there are enough men to go around."

She sniffs bitterly. "I'm not daddy's little girl. Get that through your fucking head."

Whoa. I hit a nerve. "No need to get pissy. You started it."

"I started it? How old are we?"

I let out a longwinded sigh. She's driving me nuts, and I want her antagonism to stop. I extend my hand. "Let's call a truce."

She hesitates but shakes my hand. Her palm is wet. My palm is dry.

"So what's this night all about?" I ask.

"Every single person who needs special attention so that we can get shit done will be in the room tonight. I have a relationship with each one of them. I know you've been wondering why my father wants you to keep me around. You're about to find out."

Politics. Vince has always been better at it than me. I respect the man who works hard to be the best, not some slimy-ass individual who relies on cronyism to get ahead. I can't scratch backs, and I sure as hell don't want mine scratched.

Grace talks about all the people she plans to introduce me to tonight. I'm certainly intrigued.

City Hall is an ostentatious building on the outskirts of downtown. Its gothic dome is lit up, which makes the structure appear as if it's a relic from Europe's past. The original City Hall, which was just as overworked design-wise, collapsed during the 1906 earthquake. This one was built in 1915. What's funny is the original structure collapsed because of cronyism and back scratching, which is why we're here tonight.

The limo stops behind a line of other limos. I want to get out of the car where we're stopped, but Grace, who's back to sending text messages, holds up her hand, shakes her head, and says, "Be patient."

It takes nearly forty-five minutes for us to get our red-carpet exit. The driver opens the door for us. We get out of the vehicle, and cameras flash.

"Mr. Tango, over here," a photographer shouts.

All of a sudden, my name is being called by so many men with cameras that I can't count them.

"What the hell is going on? Why the fuck do they know who I am?" I say to Grace.

"I sent out a press release," she says through a pasted-on smile.

My name is still being called, and I don't like the sound of it. This shit just got real. I keep my face forward. I've never been the type to play to the cameras. The last time these fuckers were interested in me, I was fucking a crazy royal chick from England. They pinned me as the bad-boy businessman from America and said that I gave that maniac chick a venereal disease. I would have never fucked her without a condom. I don't even know why I fucked her in the first place. I think I went on a binge and was high for the whole month we were together—but not too stoned to forget to wear a condom. I knew her reputation.

Grace keeps up the fake smile. "Look into those cameras and smile your ass off."

"This is your game, not mine." I continue to face forward.

"Fuck you, Tango."

"You're not my type," I say, but I wish I could take the words back just as fast as I say them.

Grace and I enter the grand doorway. She's silent as we weave through the crowd, still arm-in-arm on our way to the ballroom.

"Listen, I didn't mean that. That was immature of me," I whisper in her ear.

"I don't want to fuck you either, Tango. But what I'm doing is protecting my father's legacy, so when I say smile at the cameras, you fucking smile at the cameras," she says past her pasted-on smile.

"All right." I paste on my own smile and turn toward the cameras. The bulbs flash.

Grace winks at me. It's apparent that she loves being in charge.

I'm shaking hands and saying the same shit over and over. I'm the new owner of Kennedy Creative. I've been in the media industry for the last eight years. Then I listen to the other person discreetly tell me what they expect from me. We arrive at our fifth councilman—Gerald Bush. I'm amused by how he chuckles after everything he says. There are two reasons why a person does that. Either they're nervous or they lie a lot. I suspect in his case, it's the latter.

"Ralph Kennedy revered the antiquity of San Francisco," he says and chuckles.

I've noticed that his chuckles linger until Grace or I start speaking.

"I'm more of a modern man," I say. "As a matter of fact, I've been thinking about making Kennedy Creative a contemporary modern firm."

Grace chastises me with a look.

Gerald Bush chuckles. "Well, contrary to the technical gold rush, Mr. Tango, San Francisco remains a city given to nostalgia."

Grace opens her mouth to speak.

"Call me Robert," I say, cutting her off. "So, Gerald"—I lean in close—"do you live in the district you represent—full-time?"

"Oh yes!" He laughs.

"Is that so? I'm sure you have more than one house in the city, don't you?" I tilt my head, a gesture that warns him to not lie to me.

"Oh yes, I invest in the right properties." He chuckles again.

I snort cynically. "Got you."

Grace's nimble fingers dig into my shoulder. "Anyway, we're looking forward to attending the

Fall Ball this year. We'll purchase the same number of seats as usual." She looks at me for consensus.

I take too long to respond, and her expression transforms into a grimace.

"Well, we'll hold the spots for you," Gerald says. He extends his hand for a final handshake.

I oblige him. "Nice meeting you."

"The pleasure was mine." There's the laugh again.

As soon as he's a safe distance away, Grace tugs on my arm. "What in the hell was that?"

I curl my arm around her waist and put my mouth to her ear. "Listen, I know what's important to that fucker, and it's not nostalgia or his Fall Ball. If I need that parasite, then I'll buy him."

Grace's mouth drops open in shock.

"Listen, I appreciate what you came here to do. I want you to keep doing it, but I've allocated over a billion dollars of capital to this company. You can buy his ten-thousand-dollars-a-plate meals and kiss his ass, but that gives him the potential to say no whenever he fucking feels like it."

Grace grunts as if she wants to negate everything I just said but then thinks better of it.

I sweep the scope of the floor with my hand. "I

do appreciate the tour, but this shit only gets you so far."

"Grace?" a man says.

Grace and I turn to look behind us. A guy about my age stands there in a suit.

Grace flinches as if she's surprised to see him. "Tyler? What are you doing here?"

Tyler watches me as though if he looks hard enough, he'll find all the answers he seeks. "The same thing you're doing here."

Grace and Tyler hug each other loosely. I'm not an intuitive man, but even I can sense the tension between them.

He extends his hand to me. "You must be the new Ralph of Kennedy Creative."

I shake his hand. "Robert Tango."

"I know. Nice to meet you. Tyler Penso."

I grimace. The name sounds familiar. "You were a principal architect for Kennedy Creative?"

He throws up his hands. "You caught me."

"Right..." I glance at Grace.

She looks as if she swallowed a canary.

"You did good work," I say.

"You looked through my projects folder?"

"I'm thorough." I'm like a shark that smells blood. "I've been meaning to call you."

He's obviously trying to fight the urge to smile. "Is that so?"

"You're a great talent. I'm sure Ralph had to let you go because he couldn't afford you but—"

"That's not why I was let go," he says, glaring at Grace.

Grace starts to say something, but her voice cracks. She clears her throat and tries again. "I'm glad you landed back on your feet."

"Right. How's Carter?" His tone is bitter.

Curiosity shoots through me like bolts of lightning. Grace glances nervously at me. She's fucking hiding something.

"Carter's doing fine," I say.

He and I lock eyes, and it's as if I'm looking through a mirror that can see past the image. He's in love with Carter, and I'm intrigued by her. I think about reneging on my plan to ask him back, but I'm not the sort of man who shuns a challenge.

"Carter's now one of our principal architects," I say.

"Oh." He looks at Grace. "I take it you didn't have anything to do with her promotion."

Grace glares at him. Now I see what's going on. Grace is definitely the one who's been holding

Carter back. She's jealous. If I think ill of her for it, that would be like me calling the tea kettle black.

"A firm is only as good as its talent," I say, choosing not to rub salt over Grace's wound. "I was hoping to convince you to return to Kennedy Creative."

He grunts, sounding intrigued. "Then I'll be expecting that call."

"Definitely."

Tyler and I shake hands again.

"Grace," he says, his tone cold.

Grace's lips are clenched tightly as she nods.

"No," she says once he's gone.

"No what?" I ask.

"He can't come back."

"That's not your call. And what in the hell is going on between the two of you?"

She shakes her head. "We'll discuss this further tomorrow."

She's so tightly wound that I choose not to have this argument with her. We continue making our way through the room, shaking hands and promising city planners, council members, and chief administrators that I'm willing to go with the program. But Grace isn't the same after our run-in with Tyler. I still wonder what the hell is going on between them, but I figure I'll get my answers in due time.

I'm up the next morning before my alarm sounds. I've never been this excited to rise and shine and get to the job. As soon as I make it to the office and sit at my desk, I'm in go mode. My first order of business is to have Zoe call Tyler and schedule an interview. In less than fifteen minutes, he's scheduled to come in this Friday.

Grace walks into my office without being asked to come in. "About Tyler—he should not be part of my father's company."

I sit back in my chair and rest my chin on the steeple I make with my fingers. "Why not?"

She closes the door and sits across from me. "He insulted my father."

"How did he insult your father?"

"My father likes manners, and Tyler will insult you too if you bring him back."

I sigh hard and shake my head. "Do you really think I'm a stupid asshole who can't read between the lines? Have you two fucked or something?"

Grace shoots to her feet. "Forget it. Do what you have to do, and I'll do the same."

"That sounds like a threat."

"Take it however you want to take it."

"Then I won't take it as a threat because you can't threaten me."

Grace stomps out of my office, and as they say, out of sight, out of mind.

As the week progresses, I finalize my contract with Ralph and keep rejuvenating his failing empire. I work day and night. Carter and I make eye contact every now and then, but there's no time for me to try to make skin-on-skin contact happen between us. By Friday, I'm wiped but ready for my sit-down with Tyler. After reviewing his old projects again, I'm willing to pay whatever it costs to have him back in our stable.

I stand in the doorway of my office when he stops at the main entrance and scans the entire floor. Carter, who's at Matt's desk, watches him in shock as he walks down the aisle. Then she looks at me with a question in her eyes.

Tyler and I shake hands. The firmness of his grip says he's here to deal and be victorious. I match his grip because I mean to do the same.

"Glad you could make it," I say.

"Always willing to entertain an offer. Although my current firm has already rewarded me for my talent," he says.

I make a mental note—he's cocky. I ask him to have a seat. Carter stares into my office as she crosses the aisle to return to her desk.

"Talent should be rewarded," I say. "But if we can't afford you, then I understand. After all, talented people are a dime a dozen, and I don't mind going fishing for them."

He pauses to survey my expression. I can't stand cockiness. I've been known to be a cocky prick every now and then, but it's a part of myself that I want to leave in the Dumpster.

Tyler looks out the window, surveying the floor. His eyes stop on Carter. "I see a lot has changed."

"All it took was five weeks, and this is only the beginning. I look forward to surpassing this firm's former glory."

Carter takes her seat, and Tyler puts his focus on me. "Didn't you come from the world of media?"

"Yes, I did." I'm getting used to answering that question.

"Then what do you know about architecture?"

"I have my credentials."

"What are they?"

"I'm not the one being interviewed. But the short of it is, I have an MFA in architecture along with an MBA in Business Administration. I completed my apprenticeship under Barney Arsenault of Customize Designs."

He sits up in his seat. "You worked directly with Arsenault?"

"Yes, I did."

"How in the hell did you swing that?"

"I'm talented—just like you."

Tyler smirks. "Okay then, let's get to the important part."

I open the offer folder Zoe compiled. Zoe's more thorough than Mavis and without the fucking superior attitude. The first offer is a lowball offer but not so low it would insult him. As expected, Tyler rejects it. I ask him to counter, and he comes up just below the amount I was prepared to pay. I appear generous when I offer him the salary I had in mind.

"That's a lot of money, Mr. Tango."

"Robert," I say, "and you're welcome. When can you start?"

"When do you need me?"

"I thought you had another job?"

I see that strained look in his eyes. He's happier than he's letting on, and there can only be one reason that could be.

I look at him suspiciously. "You don't have another job?"

"No."

"You knew I would be at City Hall on Monday night?"

He shows me his cocky smirk again. "Perhaps. Someone told me you might be looking to hire some of us back, and I wanted to be the first."

I'm impressed by his boldness. "Well, then you're the first."

Then we negotiate his position. He agrees to start as another principal architect. He wanted to become chief principal architect, but I suspected he merely wanted to be over Carter. There's something going on between Carter, Tyler, and Grace.

Tyler will start tomorrow morning. When I catch the strange look on Zoe's face as she watches him leave, I ask her into my office.

"How did it go?" she asks as soon as she takes a seat.

"It went well." I show her the kind of smile that normally puts her at ease. "Hopefully I'm not over-stepping my boundaries if I ask you this, but I sense tension between Carter and Grace, and I think it has something to do with the man who just left this office."

Zoe sighs and rolls her eyes as if she can finally let go of what's been troubling her. She doesn't take many pauses as she recounts how Carter and Tyler used to date. They were pretty hot and heavy. Zoe thinks they were together for two years. Then he cheated on her with Grace. However, the rumor was he did it because Ralph favored Carter as an architect and everyone thought that he would promote her to a principal before Tyler. When Carter found out he had cheated with Grace, she was devastated.

"There was nothing gracious about the way Grace flaunted their relationship. That's kind of why Carter stays in her corner and talks to no one."

"I see her talking to Matt." I desperately want to know what's really going on between the two of them. I've pictured Matt fucking her, and it drove me crazy.

Zoe rolls her eyes a little. "Oh, Matt. He's had a crush on her forever, like most of the guys around here."

I detect resentment in her tone. "I see…"

"Anyway, that's not the end of the story. After

Tyler was promoted, he started up with Carter again. He was seeing them both at the same time."

She explains how when Grace found out, she wanted to have Carter fired, but Ralph wouldn't allow it. However, Grace made things as difficult as she could for Carter. She gave her the worst assignments, which lowered her rate of commission.

"She basically tried to starve Carter out. Then there were rumors of financial instability, and layoffs soon followed." Zoe grunts thoughtfully. "Once again, Grace tried to convince Ralph to let go of Carter, but in a surprising twist, Ralph fired Tyler. Shocked all of us."

I tap my fingers on my desk as I ponder. I wonder if bringing Tyler back into the fold was a good idea. "Thanks, Zoe. That'll be all for now."

Zoe stands, walks to the door, then turns to face me. "I want to say thank you for making this place what it is now. Everybody's excited to come to work everyday. It hasn't been this way in a long time, and for some, never. And everybody here respects you. And, um, if I may…"

"You may," I say.

"I see the way Carter looks at you and vice versa. It's so easy to lose respect around here, you know?" Her facial expression says it all.

I glance at where Carter sits. We had fun at lunch last Friday, and I want to spend more time off the clock with her. She's constantly on my mind. I've been in an embittered battle between maintaining my integrity as the man in charge and my desire to be in her presence. I hate that Matt and now Tyler were allowed to make an effort to be with her, but I can't. I haven't forgotten the harsh opinion Maggie and Mavis had of me. It wouldn't have been so impactful if I hadn't been fucking a chick whose name I never knew when I overheard them. What Zoe just said abolishes the shame and disappointment within me. There are plenty of fish in the sea. Carter is one that I've caught but I'm forced to release back into the ocean. I choose duty over desire.

8

SOUL PROPRIETOR

THREE MONTHS LATER

*T*he conference room erupts in applause. The entire company is gathered together. We're one hundred fifty-three employees strong, and I try to take in as many faces as possible. To think, three months ago, I was rich in resources but poor in self-worth and faith in my future.

Yesterday, Richard Darling and I spent the afternoon at Ralph's lawyer's office, finalizing the sale of Kennedy Creative. I sat back and let Richard do most of the talking. Ralph and I were in agreement on all the terms except one, and when Richard lowered the boom, Ralph could hardly believe it.

"Regarding the name of the company," Richard

said. "My client is allowed to add subsidiaries, giving them equal weight as Kennedy Creative."

Ralph looked at his lawyer for clarification, and he explained that I could create subsidiaries to the architecture firm and assign them functions at will. Ralph glared at me as if he wanted to rip off my head.

I said, "I'll respect the initial objectives of the company."

"Which are?" Ralph's posture indicated that he thought I was bullshitting him.

"Integrity first," I said, although the shit he'd pulled with the interest payment wasn't very scrupulous.

Ralph and I engaged in a stare-off.

Richard put the finalized document in front of me to sign. "I'm sure Mr. Kennedy doesn't mind a little name change. He just got a half a billion dollars richer today." He winked at Ralph. "Collecting all of that interest money my client refuses to contest."

That was a point that needed to be made. Ralph took the snide out of his grin, shook my hand, and wished me luck.

At this very moment, as I stand in front of my entire enterprise and run the state-of-the-company meeting, I can happily say that this all belongs only to me.

I've just finished giving them the rundown, including why we're operating in the black even after losing Ralph's capital. Last month, our acquisitions team submitted bids for eight of the most coveted projects in the city, and we've heard back from seven out of eight. We were chosen to represent all of the projects, and there's a good chance that we'll receive the eighth as well. The room erupts in applause once again. I notice how the project teams eye each other. They all want the most expensive account, and I've developed a system where the only way to be rewarded is by merit and not favoritism.

I lift my hand to quiet them down. "We've slaved like hell in the last three months. Some of you have gone for weeks working fifteen-hour days, which doesn't leave much time for fun or sleep." I raise my hand. "I'm guilty."

There's laughter. I adopted the motto that I'm the first to arrive and the last to leave. I'm not sure if it's because I don't want to be perceived as a failure, but I never let my employees out-work me.

I wait until they quiet down to deliver the next much-needed news. "And that is why this Monday and Tuesday, we're closed for business. I want you all to take a four-day weekend to try to reclaim your lives."

The applause isn't so loud this time.

"Whoa, I think I've created a bunch of worka-holics!" I smile as a rumble of laughter fills the room. "I realize your minds are heavy with all of the shit that you have to get done; mine is too. But I've always respected the idea of work-life balance, and we're all way out of balance. And don't worry, you're still getting paid."

They laugh again.

I allow myself to finally glance at Carter. Just like everyone else in the room, she's watching me. It's been a while since I focused on her face, and it takes a moment before I realize that my eyes have lingered for too long on her. I look down at the lectern and clear my throat. When I lift my face, I'm grinning big.

I look at my wristwatch. "It's Friday, 1:48 p.m. I'm closing shop early, so go home. Our clients will hear and see you all on Wednesday morning!"

I take in the last round of applause. The sound reverberates through me like the melodies of a full orchestra. I would've never believed that I could earn this sort of adulation without being Vince's sidekick.

MY EMPLOYEES quickly trickle out of the building. I apparently don't have to tell them twice to call it a day. I, on the other hand, have a lot of work to finish up before embarking on the four-day weekend.

I'm typing on my computer when an envelope is thrown on my desk. I look up. It's Grace.

I throw up my hands. "What the hell?"

She closes my office door. "You want favors from those people, then I want Carter out of here."

I open the envelope mainly out of curiosity, and I read the names. I snort cynically. Gerald Bush is on the list, but a handful of key names are missing, and one of them is Jack Lord.

I fold the page, stuff it back into the envelope, open my desk drawer, and put it away. "You know what I think? I think someone has convinced you that I'm a buffoon. You think I'm going to crack and binge on young, hot employee sex and cocaine before I run this company into the ground."

She snarls. "Young, hot sex and cocaine? Is that what you're addicted to?"

I glare at her with narrowed eyes. "I wanted to respect your father, but you've made that impossible. You're fired. Get the hell out of my building."

She squares her shoulders as if she's ready to rumble. "You can't fire me!"

"I can, and I have." I pick up my desk phone. "Do I have to call security?"

"Those people on that list will make sure you never get clearance for the permits you need, or any other kind of agency approvals."

My expression is as cold as ice. "You're bored, Grace. Get the fuck out of my office."

She shakes her head as though she's been struck by shock. "Wait. I mean it, Robert. Those people are very important to my father's operation, and you need them and me."

"I'm also bothered by the fact that you can't seem to remember that I made your father a half a billion dollars richer and now I own this company. Why don't you go ask him for some of it and go lie on a beach in Tahiti or somewhere?"

"Ha!" she scoffs.

"Okay, make it Mars, but regardless, I need you to get the fuck out of my presence." I've become slightly distracted by the email that just popped up on my screen. It reminds me what I was doing before Grace walked in here with her troth of bullshit to shove down my throat. I type on my computer as I say, "You have until I finish answering this email to get out of here, or I'm calling security."

Grace has become an enemy, and one never tells the enemy why their strike didn't draw blood. I'm richer and more connected than she is. The people on her list will ultimately answer to the highest authority—my cash. Grace has proven to me that even women can be narcissistic idiots who think their strategic charisma is all it takes to dominate. She's a star in her own mind—powerful in a pea-sized universe.

Although I don't look up, I sense that she's turned her back to leave.

"I don't ever want to see you again," I say.

I wait for her to get the hell out of my office, but she stands still. I look up. Her entire body is shaking. I don't want to be sympathetic to whatever's going on with her at the moment. She came in here with both guns blazing, took her best shots, and didn't even graze the target. Now she should go lick her wounds like an adult and move on. But she's wearing another tight red dress that shows off her tits, along with a pretty face and tears trapped in her eyes. Those are the best powers of influence she has to use against a guy like me.

"What is it?" I ask harshly.

She puts a hand over her mouth and shakes her head.

"Do you need a moment?"

She nods. It's awkward as hell. I did not expect this show of weakness from Grace.

"I need you to rethink your decision to fire me," she says.

"If you were me, would you trust you after the stunt you just pulled?" I ask.

She stares at me pleadingly. This has to be a game she's playing.

"I thought so," I say.

"I'm sorry," she says.

"I accept your apology, but I can never trust you again. I wish you luck though."

"It's just…"

I set my gaze. Even a fool can see that there's no changing my mind.

"I just can't stand that he chose her over me. That's all."

"If jealousy can make you pull a stunt like this, then maybe you should seek help."

She wipes her eyes. "I guess I should."

Whether she's fucking with me or not, seeing her in this state makes me empathetic. "I'm not being facetious. Get help, then maybe we can talk in the future. Your father built this company from the ground up. It would be a shame if you weren't part of its future, but after what you pulled, I need some assurance that I can trust you."

We stare at each other. Grace finally turns and walks out of my office. She proceeds slowly down the aisle, keeping her head up. Carter hasn't left yet, and I wait to see if Grace shoots her a final glare. She doesn't, and I'm thankful. After she's gone, Carter looks toward the exit then at me. We lock gazes. She's the first to let go. Shit, I think she took my breath away.

I stay at my work for a while. Zoe was one of the first to leave. She wanted to stay, but I insisted that she leave. If anyone has pulled more than their share, it's Zoe. I've been trying to figure out a way to reward her for the work she has done. Ralph had given her the job title of administrative assistant. I've considered changing her title to executive assistant and tripling her salary, but I haven't yet spoken to her about where she sees herself in the next five years. The last thing I put on my calendar is "Meeting w/Zoe." It's set for nine Wednesday morning.

I rub my eyes and look at the time on the computer screen. It's ten thirty at night. It's time to return to the hotel. I have a busy weekend ahead of me, including house hunting and having one of my cars transported from LA to San Francisco. I believe I waited so long to handle these details because deep down, I thought I would fail at making this company float. I'm learning to never doubt myself again.

I yawn. That's the final sign that it's time to go. I power off my computer, turn off my desk light, and gather my things. The main floor light is off, which means everyone has left. As soon as I step out of my office, the main floor light turns on, and I nearly jump out of my skin. Carter is still in her chair with her face resting on her desk. She's asleep.

I walk over and stand above her for a moment. She has the prettiest face. I don't want to disturb her, but I can't leave her here alone. I touch her shoulder. "Carter?"

She wakes with a start. "Shit…"

"You fell asleep," I say.

"I did." She rubs her eyes. "Shit, I was just…"

I wait for her to finish whatever she was going to say, but she doesn't. Instead, she looks me in the eyes. Her pretty face makes me smile.

Carter shakes her head. "Nothing, I was just working."

"No plans for the long weekend?" I ask.

She yawns. "I've got nothing. What about you?"

I'm surprised she asked me that so casually. She's normally nervous around me. "I'm going to move out of that goddamn hotel. I have a friend who's going to let me stay in his house until I buy my own."

She perks up a little. "You're going house hunting?"

I'm entranced by the sparkle in her eyes. "Yes," I say breathlessly. "Do you want to come with me?" Shit, that slipped out.

"Are you serious?"

Extremely. "Yeah. Sure. Yes."

"Okay then." She smiles. "I know of some great homes on the market that will suit your taste."

I grunt, intrigued. "What do you know about my taste?" My heart skips a beat. I've been waiting for Carter to bat her eyelashes at me like that for the longest time.

"More than you think," she says.

I know that I'm smirking. I want her to see that I'm thinking naughty thoughts about her. "Then lay it on me?"

"You're a contemporary man but in the way that you like new materials." She shakes her head. "No… you like to take the old and reform it into something that has never existed."

"But there's nothing new under the sun."

"Exactly. But you don't mind giving it the old college try."

I want to kiss her, but instead I bite my lower lip. "Get your things. I'll walk you out."

Her smile is full of warmth. "That's okay. I'm going to stay and work for a little while longer."

"Oh yeah, what are you working on?"

She follows my line of sight to her desk. There's nothing in front of her. As far as I can tell, she hasn't been working on anything but sleep.

"I was just taking a break." She lifts the top of her desk and takes out a drafting pad. "You gave me the Wilmore Estate. I was working on some options for the upstairs."

She's nervous, and I also suspect that she's lying.

"That can wait until Wednesday, can't it?" I say.

"I feel inspired now. I don't want to lose momentum."

I still sense that she's more stressed than she's letting on, but I don't push. "Okay. Have a good night."

"I will," she says with another yawn.

"Good night then."

"Good night."

Our gazes linger. I don't want to leave her. I take a few steps away then stop.

"Are you sure you have no plans for the week-end?" I ask. My heart is racing like a locomotive. This isn't like me. I'm never nervous around women.

Her eyes expand. "I'm sure."

Oh shit, I can't believe I'm about to ask her this. "I'm staying at my house in Napa…"

"You have a house in Napa?"

"Yeah," I say with a grin. "I was wondering if you wanted to come up. Maybe we can go house hunting from there."

I anxiously await her reply. Her pretty face is so tired. She even has dark circles around her eyes.

"Sure, absolutely," she says.

"Good. Then I'll pick you up at around eight in the morning. What's your address?"

She looks off to think. "You can just pick me up here."

I grimace. "Here?"

"Yes."

I wonder why she doesn't want me to see where she lives. I don't think she lives with a boyfriend or else she wouldn't spend the weekend with me. Regardless, I don't think I should stick my nose in where it doesn't belong.

"Here at eight?" I say.

She musters up a smile and nods.

"See you then," I say.

We smile at each other one last time, and I leave her alone, which I don't feel good about at all.

I get into my car and head back to the hotel, but I can't help worrying about Carter. Something's going on with her, and she's hiding it from me. I remember that she and Allie used to be pretty close. I want to call Allie and ask if there's anything going on with Carter. I haven't paid much attention to Carter in the last two months. Ignoring her was easy to do while working fifteen- to twenty-hour days. It was only during my hour-long workouts at the gym or when I beat off that thoughts of her creeped into my head.

As I drive along, I try to figure out why I like *her*

out of all the women I've encountered in the last three months. April and Celia have been sending me emails, inviting me to different events and asking how my day is going. I've ignored most of their messages. Ignoring them became easier once their project was completed and their invoices paid. The next time they want to use Kennedy Creative, their fee will be twice the usual amount. They got a deal for all the headaches they caused Carter. But that's the nature of cronyism. Those two women are Grace's friends. Grace is another woman I would've gladly fucked three months ago. She's hot and powerfully sexy. I used to love chasing the difficult ones and making the easy ones wait. What a tool I was. I don't want to play those damn games with myself or with Carter. One look at her face, and I feel as if I've known her all my life.

That look on her face… the exhaustion in her eyes… where was her helmet?

CARTER

As soon as Robert left, Carter dropped her head back on the desk. She was so sleepy that she could hardly keep her eyes open. Not only that, but she couldn't believe she'd said yes to spending the weekend with him. How many times had she hoped he would walk up to her desk and ask her out? The answer was every day since their lunch at Yao Fun. One look at Robert, and she wanted to tell him everything. It probably was presumptuous of her, but Carter felt as if Robert could fix the turmoil she was going through. All she had to do was tell him the truth. Why hadn't she said anything? Maybe because she didn't believe in fairy tales. "Prince Charming" was the reason she was in this situation in the first place. Only her Prince Charming had turned into the ugly frog.

Carter yawned and slid off her chair. She headed to Robert's office. This would be the third night in a row that she'd slept on the sofa in his office. It was actually more comfortable than her bed, yet she still missed her lumpy bed. Carter also missed taking a steaming hot shower. For the last three days, she had taken a birdbath in the ladies' room. She could've stayed in a hotel, but that would have felt too much like admitting defeat.

Tonight she was too exhausted to try to figure out how she had landed in such a bad situation and what was the best way out of it. One big decision she had to make was if she was ready to leave San Francisco for good. Perhaps she'd let her thoughts torture her when she woke up at six in the morning. She woke up at that time every morning, like clockwork. Carter closed her eyes, and before long, she had drifted off to sleep.

"HEY…" she heard.

Carter remained stuck between conscious and unconsciousness.

"Carter?"

She took some deep breaths and rubbed her eyes until they opened. The light in Robert's office was on, and he was standing over her.

9

WHAT'S IN A WEEKEND

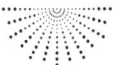

*C*arter sits up. "Robert?" She's still rubbing her eyes.

"What are you doing here?" I ask.

She stands, and her legs are wobbly. I catch her and hold her steady.

"I'm sorry, I'll leave."

Suddenly I realize that she's embarrassed. Tears are rolling from her eyes.

"You don't have to leave." I keep my tone earnest. "But I would like to know what's going on with you." I wipe a tear from the corner of her eye.

Her lips part, and her warm breath tickles my chin. I want to kiss her so badly. My dick stiffens. I swallow, take deep breaths, and get control of my lust.

She closes her eyes. "It just…"

"Just what?"

She sits on the sofa and pats the space beside her. I sit.

"Have you heard about Tyler and me?"

I wish I could say no. "I've heard some things."

She looks as if she didn't want me to say that. "Oh…"

I rub her hand. "It's okay. What does Tyler have to do with you sleeping in my office?" I feel the tension in my lips. I don't know how he put her in this situation, but I want to rip his head off for it.

"We used to live together. He moved out, but his name was on the lease. On Monday, he made the landlord kick me out. I asked if I could take over the lease, and she said no." She shakes her head. "It's him. He just wants to stick it to me."

"Okay then, tomorrow morning we'll go and get your place back."

"No, that's okay. The memories… I just need time."

I study her with a frown. I can see how confused she is. "Time for what?"

She heaves a long sigh. "To figure it all out."

I can see in her eyes that she's hiding something else from me. "Well, where are your things?"

"In my car."

"Your car? I thought you drove a motorcycle?"

"Only in the summer."

I smile and pat her thigh. "Well, let's get up and go."

She looks panicked again. "Go where?"

"I would say to my hotel room, but I know how that would look. Let's just drive out to Napa tonight."

"Tonight?"

"Tonight. It's not that far."

Her eyebrows ruffle. "Are you sure?"

I stand and offer her my hand. She takes it, and I help her to her feet.

"Let's go get your things out of your car."

We stare deeply into each other's eyes. Damn, I want that kiss, but instead I get a grip and control myself.

"I have to get my coat," she says.

We go to her desk, and she takes a black winter coat out of her storage cabinet. Once she's ready, she stands next to me. I put my arm around her waist, and she rests her head on my shoulder as we walk out of the building. The night is cold and it's raining, but neither of us increases our pace to stay warm and dry. The smell of her skin drives me crazy. I wonder if she's comfortable with me holding her this close. She hasn't tried to pull away, so I guess she's fine with it. We make it to the parking structure and take the elevator to the second level where I'm parked.

I walk her to the passenger side of my car, open the door, and she gets in. I already miss her soft, warm body against mine. We smile at each other before I close the door. Her eyes are so tired. I can't wait to make it to Napa and tuck her into one of the beds. I've spent weekends at the house for the last two and a half months, so I know it's guest-friendly and the refrigerator is stocked.

Carter forces her eyes to stay open as she directs me to a midsized sedan, which is parked on the third level of the employees' lot. I stop behind her car. She sighs and opens her door.

I put my hand on her shoulder. "Stay in."

She watches me with a quizzical expression.

"I'll get your things. Are they in the trunk?"

Carter blinks her heavy eyelids. "Yes, they are." She sounds beat.

She takes her keys out of her coat pocket and hands them to me. I keep the heater running as I get out. I take three large suitcases out her trunk. There are three plastic bags back there as well. I turn to Carter and point at the bags, but she's good and asleep. I take the bags, put all of her things in my trunk, get in, and drive off.

She only wakes up when I reach the entrance of the hotel. I roll her window down to tell the valet that he doesn't need to get up because I'm checking out. I ask Carter to stay in the car as I go inside to get my luggage and pay my bill. She nods and goes right back to sleep.

About twenty minutes later, I'm back with my suitcase and slightly annoyed after paying the final bill. I could've bought a nice house with the cash I wasted staying at that hotel. But I'm too happy Carter is in my car to sulk about the bill for too long.

Once I get past the construction, the road to Napa is clear. I zoom up the Bay Bridge Interstate 80. I keep the stereo off in order to hear Carter gently snoring. Every now and then, I glance at her heart-shaped face and pouty lips. She's just so pretty. How could I have not noticed her looks when I was fifteen? Maybe it was because she was too young and I always had a thing for the unget-table girls. Back then, that was college girls.

I'm tired and buzzed from excitement. I roll into Napa and up the road toward my house, which is nestled against the top of the mountain. I've become fond of the Spanish-style villa that I bought on a fluke. I've hired landscapers to dress the lawns and keep the trees and shrubs pruned. A few weeks ago, the entire property got a fresh coat of paint. I had the shutters changed and added decorative tiles around the arched entryways. I installed warm lighting inside and outside. Now when I drive up the path to my house and take in the ambiance, it feels more like home.

I drive up the red brick driveway, stop in front of the door, and touch Carter on the shoulder. "Hey."

She squirms, moans, and slowly opens her eyes. She perks up when she sees my house. "Oh my God."

"We're here," I say.

"Have I been asleep this whole time?"

"You have had a tough night. Come on, let's get you inside."

She rubs her eyes as she studies my house. "You live here?"

"So far only on the weekends."

"It's breathtaking."

"How about I give you a tour in the morning?"

She musters a smile. "I'd love that."

I'm captivated by her smile. "Me too."

My heart is beating a mile a minute. In order to make it stop, I remind myself that she's my employee and Vince's younger cousin and I'm a changed man. All I want to do is open her door, pick her up, run into the house, throw her on my bed, pull her jeans off, and taste her wet pussy. I want to make Carter scream and clutch the sheets like she never has before.

I take one deep breath and get out of the car. I walk around the back of the car, which is kind of hard to do with a stiff dick. I open her door. I notice her staring at my swollen cock.

"I'll get you settled in a guest room then bring your things into the house," I say.

Carter is still distracted by my cock. "Right."

I wonder what she's thinking.

CARTER

Robert took Carter by the hand and helped her to her feet. She had never felt so horny. What a big dick he had. Carter could only imagine how it would feel filling her up. They would certainly have sex—if not tonight, then soon. She was determined to make it happen. As he closed the car door, she purposely bumped her ass against his bulge. It was rock hard.

Robert stepped back as if the contact frightened him. His reaction caught her off guard. She concluded that he probably was being nice to her because she was Vince's cousin and he considered her family. After they'd had lunch that afternoon, nothing had changed between them. At times she thought she caught him staring at her, but then once she was in the break room when Rachael had told Laura that she had caught him looking at her ass. She sounded pretty excited about it.

Laura primped in the mirror. "Don't think you're special. He looks at my ass too."

When Carter walked out of the stall, both women looked at her and rolled their eyes. Carter had never seen Robert look at anyone's ass, but it hurt to hear that Robert Tango was interested in other women. As good-looking as he was, he wouldn't be single for long, and she would be fooling herself if she believed he was celibate.

Carter couldn't think of much to say as Robert helped her up the steps. His arm was around her waist again. If only he knew the mixed messages he was sending by holding her that way. They entered the house. The lighting in the hallways was warm and inviting. She'd always known Robert Tango was an impeccable man. He was rich, smart, classy, and so good-looking that the heavens sang when all of his gorgeousness entered the room.

Earlier she had rested her head on his shoulder, but that was because she was too tired to walk without his help. Carter's head was still light with exhaustion, but if Robert wanted to make love to her, she would gladly be on full alert for that. He walked her down a set of steps and into a massive bedroom. The bed, chest of drawers, nightstands, and the rest of the furnishings were all proof of his impeccable contemporary taste.

Robert walked her to the foot of the bed. "Welcome to your digs."

Carter noticed the view of downtown. The scent of Robert's skin lingered in the air. She could tell he'd spent a lot of time in that bedroom. "Is this the master bedroom?" She couldn't believe he would let her sleep in his best room.

Robert winked. "All of the rooms in this house are masters." He took a remote control off the nightstand. "Use this to lower the blackout shades."

When he handed Carter the remote, their

fingers touched. She thought she would faint from desire.

Robert pointed toward the right. "The bathroom's that way. There are fresh towels hanging up. Soap, shampoo, everything you might need is in there, but let me know if anything's missing."

Carter took note of the suggestive look in his eyes. Yes, something was missing. He was missing!

"I will," she said as calmly as she could.

He smirked and walked out of the bedroom. Carter had to flop down on the foot of the bed to gather her bearings.

ROBERT

I bring two of Carter's suitcases into my bedroom. I couldn't put Carter into one of the ordinary guestrooms; she's too special for that. All four of the bedrooms in this house are masters, but this one has the best view. I set her suitcases against the wall. The water is running in the shower, and steam trickles out of the bathroom. She left the door open. I'm tempted to see if I can get a sneak peek of her naked body.

"Fuck, what's wrong with me?" I mumble.

I rush back upstairs to get the rest of her things. I hate seeing all of her shit up against the wall. I'll email the maid service and ask them to send Sylvia in the morning to help Carter go through her things and pick out what she needs for the long weekend, then I'll store the rest.

I've made my third run, and Carter is still in the shower. It would've been nice to see her before I head to my home office. I close the door to the bedroom and leave her in peace. Exhaustion washes over me as I walk down the hallway. I go to my office and send that email to my maid service. Then I see an email from Jack Lord. His wife is opening a bakery, and he wants to know if I can drive down to Santa Barbara next weekend to assess the space. My answer is short. *"Absolutely. Reply with address and time?"*

I print the expansion report from my business development department. Without a presence in New York, we're just peons. With a presence in New York, we put ourselves in the position to become giants. I'm tempted to read the report tonight, but I'm just too tired. I save it for the morning. However, I open another email—it's from Grace. She wants to have lunch on Monday and talk to me about returning to Kennedy Creative.

I close the email. I'm in the process of changing the name of the company, not to RT Creative but to RT Modern Design. However, I'm not releasing the name Kennedy Creative. I've read Grace's employee profile. She's an interior designer, but somewhere along the way, she fell into trying to keep her father's business afloat. When she can prove that she's done being a brat, then I have a proposition for her.

She's contacting me a lot sooner than I expected, but I decide to respond to her email anyway. *Call Zoe and schedule a one-hour meeting for next week.* I cc Zoe on the email. Maybe my proposition can be incentive for her to see a shrink.

I power off my computer and head downstairs to the bedroom next door to Carter's. I pass Carter's door on the way, and strangely, the shower is still running. I stop a few feet away, worried that maybe she slipped and fell. I step back to knock on the door. Of course she wouldn't be able to hear me. I open the door.

"Carter?" I call.

The water turns off, but she doesn't say anything.

"Sorry, I was just checking to make sure you're okay," I say.

"Um..."

I hear the shower door open. I'm not sure if I should leave or not.

"I'm fine." She steps out of the bathroom, wrapped in a towel. Her hair is wet, and the sight of her slippery skin turns me the fuck on.

There's only one reason a woman lets me see her looking that way—she wants me to seduce her. I struggle to keep the former Robert Tango contained. If I fuck her, then what? She becomes my girlfriend? My lover? How will it look to the other employees? I don't know why, but I suspect they're all waiting for me to slip and fall into one of my underlings' pussy. I've seen more cleavage, nipples, and panty-less asses in the past three months than I have in my whole life, and that's saying a hell of a lot. I salivate at her milky, smooth cleavage. I could really show Carter the time of her life if I let it happen—but I won't.

"Good," I say and get the hell out of there.

Once again, I'm walking with a stiff cock. I go inside my room, shut the door, lean against it, and close my eyes to steady myself. That was close.

I hope to hell she's not persistent enough to

knock on my door. If she is, then I'll open it and fuck her brains out. I wait, feeling equal amounts of hope and dread. At least a minute goes by, and I step away from the door. I strip off my trousers, unbutton my shirt, keep on my underwear and T-shirt, and climb under the covers of my bed. I stare at the remote control that lowers the blackout shades. My brain wants me to take it and lower the shades so that the glare from the city light flowing into the sky won't disturb my sleep. However, I close my eyes, and I'm out like a lamp.

DINGY DAYLIGHT FILLS THE ROOM. I scramble to sit up. I kick myself for not setting the alarm on my cell phone. My head is still a tad bit foggy from oversleeping when I scoot off the bed, retrieve my pants from the floor, and take my cell phone out of the pocket. "Hot damn."

It's ten thirty in the morning. I vaguely remember falling asleep with a serious hard-on. Carter had walked out of the shower wearing nothing but a towel. She tempted me, and I was victorious. Fucking her would be the wrong thing to do. I slap myself upside my thick head in hopes that that fact will seep through.

Now that my head is clear, I take a quick shower and put on fresh clothes. I keep it casual—jeans and a long-sleeved V-neck sweater. I plan to take Carter into town for brunch before heading out on our house-hunting trip, but not before I show her my Harley. One step into the hallway, and I'm struck by the aroma of breakfast. Then I remember Sylvia's here this morning. Sometimes she cooks my meals. She's always asking when I'm going to get a wife to take care of me. I usually joke and tell her that I'd rather give all of my money to her. She blushes, and that's usually the end of it until the next time she comes in early and the house feels too still and lonely to her. I practically skip to the kitchen, glad she made breakfast.

"Carter?" I say, surprised to see her at the stove.

"Are you hungry?" Her tone is light and cheery.

"Where's Sylvia?"

"Oh, the woman who was supposed to help me fold my clothes and put them away?"

I shrug.

"I told her she could go home. She was very happy that you had a woman in the house though."

I lean on the frame that separates the kitchen

from the dining room. "How long have you been up?

Carter flips a pancake. "Usually I wake up at six, but I slept so good last night that I woke up at eight!" She sounds pretty proud of that.

I'm happy she's happy. "I just didn't want you to live out of your suitcases and bags the entire weekend."

"Pretty pathetic, huh?" She flips another pancake.

"It makes me want to punch Tyler in the throat, but I'll settle for firing his arrogant ass."

She almost panics. "No, you can't do that, not because of me."

"I've been looking for a reason. He's a fucking prima donna, and he's rude to my clients."

"He's rude to everybody. How do you like your eggs?"

I'm amused by her chirpy mood. I try to keep my eyes off of her tight tank top and her tight sweatpants that display the V of her pussy.

"Sunny-side up, and yes, I know he's rude to everybody. I think that's why Ralph fired his ass."

"Maybe rudeness is the price of talent."

I grunt. "No, it isn't. You're more talented than he is, and you have zero amount of ego. Why don't you strut around like a peacock like the rest of them?"

She puts three pancakes on a plate and pours more batter. "You do eat three, don't you?"

I shrug. "Sure."

"And I'm not a peacock because I don't need to be in order to feel good about myself. Underneath all the feathers are insecure people."

I grunt thoughtfully. She nailed it. I was a peacock for so many years, hiding my shitty abandonment issues and insecurity under a gang of feathers. "All right, I won't fire him yet, but if he's rude to another one my clients or employees, then his ass is out."

She grins and cracks an egg into the skillet. "Did I already say that this is a beautiful house?"

I like the way she changed the subject. "I've done some work on it in the last three months."

She sighs gravely. "Sorry about that. Avoidance. I'm very good at it."

I grin. "It's fine."

"I know that Tyler can be a certified jerk, but he is an exceptional architect."

"And so are you."

"But isn't it always good to have more than one

185

exceptional architect? You never know when one of us will have to leave."

I flinch. "Are you going somewhere?"

She turns her back to me to flip the pancakes. "I know Grace wants me gone."

"Grace? I fired her."

"But I heard that she wants to come back. She'll never stop trying to get you to re-hire her."

I think about the email she sent me. "Don't worry about it, Carter. She can't do anything to you."

Her smile says how appreciative she is that I'm willing to protect her from the crazy shit that went on at Kennedy Creative before I took over.

I wink at her and roll up my sleeves. "What can I do to help?"

"You can make coffee," she says.

I walk to the cupboard where I keep the coffee. "Making coffee."

We finish preparing breakfast, and soon we're in the dining room. I'm sitting in front of two eggs sunny-side up, a stack of three pancakes, three strips of bacon, coffee, and orange juice. Carter has made two pancakes, scrambled eggs, and two strips of bacon. I reveal to her that I have a Harley in the garage and ask if she wants to take it out today.

"Who's going to drive, you or me?" she asks.

"Um, me."

"We should flip a coin," she says.

We grin at each other.

"No need. You can drive. I'll ride bitch."

She laughs. "There's no way Robert Tango can ever ride bitch. For you, we'll call it riding stud."

I toss my head back and bellow. "All right, I'll ride stud."

We finish breakfast. I clean the kitchen as Carter goes to her bedroom to get appropriately dressed for a motorcycle ride. I avoid admiring her ass as she goes. I put the dishes and pans in the dishwasher and wipe down the counters and stove. By the time I hang the damp dishtowel on the rack, Carter's back in the kitchen. Her sexiness is effortless. I find myself yet again avoiding the desire to salivate over her hips, ass, and long legs in those tight jeans.

"You look good," I say, keeping my eyes on her face.

She winks. "So do you."

I grin. She's been flirting with me ever since last night, and it's working. "Ready for the tour?"

Again, she looks at me with smoldering eyes. "I'm ready when you are."

I ignore the desire to pull her against my chest and make out with her. Instead, I take her to the backyard garden. The trimmed shrubs and cobblestone pathways impress her. Carter sits on one of the iron benches, and I sit beside her.

She's soaking in the ambiance. "Do you plan to keep living here on the weekends?"

"Sure, why not? I've been cooped up in LA and New York for so long that I forgot how it felt to have space."

"Do you know exactly which San Francisco neighborhood you want to live in?"

I smirk. "Since you know me so well, can you guess?"

She shows me that seductive look again. "San Francisco is loaded with Victorians, Edwardians, and Tudors of every size, shape, and style. I don't see you living in one of those."

"Me neither."

She narrows an eye. "Hmm... Twin Peaks West?"

I'm taken aback. "Get the hell out of here."

"No?"

"No, it's yes!"

"You're interested in the mid-century Moderns?"

"Damn skippy. I'm partial to the Eichler homes."

Carter nods as she ponders. "Three are for sale at the moment. One of them is half-renovated. The owner ran out of money, but the price is still too high. It's been on the market the longest and has the best views. After you see it, you'll want it."

"You sound sure of yourself," I say.

She pats my thigh. "That's because I am sure of myself."

"All right then. Let's get on the bike and go."

Carter hops to her feet. "The suspense is killing me."

I lead her to the garage, which sits on the outer edge of the garden. I open the barn doors, and Carter walks in. She observes the tools that hang neatly on the wall, my masonry workbench with an electric saw that I use mainly to cut wood for the fireplace, then she looks at the shiny concrete floor.

"Wow, it's clean in here."

I walk to my bike. "There's no use in keeping it dirty."

"You're so meticulous. From the way you have your shampoo and soap placed in the shower, to the way you have items placed in the refrigerator and cabinets, and now this."

I watch her with a weak smile. I've never given my habits any thought. But now that I think about it, my ex-wife, Lena, used to give me shit about being too orderly. She said my space was the only thing I could control while I let the rest of my life fall to pieces, including our six-year marriage. Lena Chance... I took things too far when I married her. I was jealous of the natural chemistry between her and Vince. I wanted his shiny object. Suddenly, I realize that I have a lot to ask Vince to forgive me for. He and his family took me in when my mother exposed me to drunk, abusive assholes. My days turned dark after my dad died, but if it weren't for the Adams, then my days would've been darker.

Carter snaps her fingers. "Robert?"

I bring myself back into the moment. "Sorry about that."

"There's no need to apologize."

I pull the cover off my motorcycle. "Ta da!"

Carter's eyes shine.

"I see you approve," I say.

She straddles the seat and arches her back seductively. "I more than approve."

Down, boy, I say to my dick. I take a deep breath to steady my desires. "Then let's get on the road before it rains."

She scoots to the back seat. "And, Robert, there's no way I'm going to waste the opportunity to be your bitch."

I laugh, but I want to lift her off that seat, lay her down on the concrete, and peel her out of her skin-tight pants. Instead, I take my riding jacket and boots out of one of the closets. They're not dusty even though I haven't worn them in years. I take two helmets out of the closet, one that fits my head and a smaller one for Carter.

I start the engine, and it's shaky. I rev it up and let it get warm. Once the motorcycle finds that sweet-sounding purr, I take off but not too fast. It would kill me if I crashed and something happened to Carter.

There's a fair share of wind but not enough to make me worry. Carter holds me tightly as I take the road out of Napa. The fields are painted green, and the mountain edges are rocky. Blessed by nature, California is a sight for sore eyes. The insects slamming against my window are the reason I stopped riding so much. Carter rests her head on my back. The way she's holding me makes me think that she feels safe.

This could be a romantic motorcycle ride all the way to the city, but by the time we turn onto the interstate, it's raining like hell and visibility is non-existent. The next exit is coming up on my right. Carter and I seem to have the same thought because she squeezes my shoulders twice, and I make the turn off the freeway. I pull into the parking lot of a fast-food restaurant and park the bike under a tree.

I take off my helmet, and Carter takes off hers. We look at each other and chuckle.

She gazes up at the sky. "I knew this would happen."

I look up. The sky is gray and hangs low. "So did I. I guess taking the bike was wishful thinking. We can still head into the city; I'll just have to drive the car." The rain pounds the ground. "And we have to wait until this dies down."

Carter gets off the motorcycle. "No, we don't. Let me drive." She's positioned to take the driver's seat.

I hesitate. "I don't know, it's coming down pretty hard."

"You know how to run a multi-million-dollar business, and I know how to ride a motorcycle." She grins.

And so I relinquish the driver's seat and ride bitch.

CARTER

When it came to motorcycles, Carter knew she was the better driver. She could've gotten them safely to San Francisco in the rain, but they would've been drenched by the time they arrived. The only reason she rolled the dice on the weather was because she wanted to finally wrap her arms around Robert's strong frame. She was sort of happy to be returning to his Napa house. Hopefully Robert would change his mind about house hunting and they could spend the day getting to know each other better. She was hoping by nightfall, they would be sharing a bed.

Her driving was smoother than Robert's, and he seemed okay with letting her take over. Tyler used to hate it when she asserted herself. Carter could've driven faster but didn't want to show off. For the first time ever, she was willing to become whatever it took to be the sole object of Robert Tango's obsession. His chest felt like heaven against her back. If only she could seep into his body. For a moment, she thought he had massaged her belly, and his touch tickled her clit. She prayed that Robert would make a move on her, but when she made it back to his house, pulled into the garage, and parked, they took off their helmets and he scurried off to get the car. She waited in the garage and out of the rain.

Carter looked at her watch. Two minutes had passed. She wondered what was taking him so long. Her cell phone rang, and the name Tyler Asshole lit the screen. She contemplated canceling the call, but she answered it anyway.

"What?" she snapped.

She heard him sigh. "I don't want to fight, Carter."

"I just asked what do you want."

"I want to know how you're doing."

She laughed bitterly. "Are you kidding me? You made my landlord throw me out of my apartment, you asshole!"

"What! No, I didn't," he said.

Carter frowned. He sounded pretty adamant about it. "Johnny said your name was on the lease and you paid to break it early as of December 15th."

Tyler fell silent.

"Just forget it. I don't want to talk to you…"

"Carter, I didn't do that. I would never do that to you."

"Who else could've done it?"

A face came to mind. Once again, Tyler fell silent. Carter knew they both were thinking of the same person.

Carter released the tension in her body and sat on a work stool. "Who, Tyler?" She wanted to hear him say it.

"I'll look into it. I'm so sorry, babe."

"I'm not your babe."

"Where are you?"

She looked around the garage. "Somewhere safe."

"Are you with Matt?"

"No, and why do you care?"

"Why didn't you say anything to me? I supposedly had you tossed out of your home, and you didn't call? Is that what you think of me?"

Carter squeezed her eyes shut. Her sinuses swelled. She didn't know if she wanted to cry from relief or anger. She was mad at herself for not confronting Tyler. If she had said something to him, maybe she wouldn't have had to sleep in the office for the last three days—and even that was a choice. She could've afforded a hotel room or to rent another place. Perhaps her choice was indicative of how her life felt at the moment, as if she were stuck in purgatory.

She hadn't ever been happy at Kennedy Creative. She was weary of San Francisco. Five months ago, she'd applied for a job in Washington, DC. She sent a follow-up email a day before Robert Tango took over Kennedy Creative, and last week, they finally got back to her. Before she was put out of her apartment, she'd had a videoconference interview with Stuart Bettie, the chief architect at Metropolis.

Yesterday, when she had returned to the apartment to get her mail, she saw a letter from Metropolis. She opened it fully expecting it to say, "Thank you for interviewing but no thanks." Instead, the letter articulated how they'd made every effort to contact her but the number on her resume was no longer active. Carter had changed her number after she broke up with Tyler because he called almost every day to check on her. They had a strange relationship, but she didn't want the man who'd left her twice for the same crazy bitch to keep calling her. Somehow he had gotten her new number and was back to calling her at least three times a week.

However, in the letter from Metropolis, Stuart Bettie had offered her the job and asked to hear back from her by next Friday. Instead of jumping in celebration, Carter had clutched her heart, feeling anxiety. Working for Robert Tango was exciting. He'd changed the entire company for the better in a matter of months. But not even the raise, job promotion, or lusting after his sexiness made her want to stay in San Francisco for another year. She would choose to stay if Robert became her lover, but how long would that last?

When Robert had announced the four-day weekend yesterday morning, her heart sank. She thought she would have to wait until Wednesday morning to see him again. But then he asked her up to his house. That was the second strike of luck she'd had in a long time. The job offer from Metropolis was the first strike.

"I don't know, Tyler. I'll call you later." Carter didn't want anything or anyone to get in the way of her plans to be intimate with Robert that weekend, and forgiving Tyler just might do the trick.

"When's later?" he asked.

"I don't know. It's just—I have to go."

"Where are you staying?"

"With a friend," she said.

"You don't have any friends."

Tyler wasn't being malicious. She didn't have one female friend in San Francisco. The women in the office were so competitive and snooty. She was hard-pressed to find one single woman her age in San Francisco, and most of the married or dating women didn't want her around their significant other. She wasn't a Jezebel, but Carter figured they didn't want their men beating off to the image of her naked or something. Sometimes she found herself hating the whole damn human race.

Robert returned carrying a large white envelope that one would keep photos in. The jovial expression that he scurried out of the garage with was gone.

"I have to go," Carter said and ended the call. She knew Tyler would call right back, so she turned off her phone. "Is everything okay?"

"You know what? How about we make this a true relaxing weekend and hang around here? I haven't shown you my secret hideaway." It appeared as if Robert was trying to banish his stressful expression with a smile, but it didn't work.

"Sure." Carter was so confused about why their plans had to change so abruptly, and she suspected it had something to do with the envelope in his hand.

10

FORBID THE FRUIT

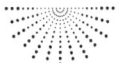

I'm working to contain my anger. I want to implode, but I promised Carter a relaxing and fun weekend, and hell if I'm going to let what I found on my front step get in the way of giving her that. She's behind me as we walk through the garden and past a wooden gate to a detached structure made of texture glass. I glance behind me to see Carter's reaction to the building. She's frowning and looking at my feet.

I stop to face her. "Hey, why the worry?"

She shrugs. "It just seems like this is all so sudden."

I look at the sky. "It stopped raining, but it'll be starting again. I want this to be a relaxing weekend like I promised."

"I consider looking at homes in San Francisco relaxing."

"Not more relaxing than this." I nod at my private oasis. I take the key out of my pocket and open the door. We walk alongside my Olympic-sized pool. "It's heating," I say.

She's looking at the envelope in my hand. "You want to go swimming?"

I tuck the envelope under my arm. "I'm just going to put this up."

"What is that?"

"Just some business that came up."

"Oh…" she says.

I point at two doors at the opposite end of the pool. "There are swimsuits in the women's room."

Carter's lips part as if she has something to say but changes her mind. I would prompt her to speak her mind, but I'm eager to make a phone call.

I take steps backward. "I'll be back shortly." I hurry out to avoid answering the perplexed look on her face.

By the time I make it to my office, I'm more pissed than I was two minutes ago. I empty the contents of the envelope on my desk. There are three photos. One is of me walking with my arm around Carter and her head on my shoulder. The anonymous sender captioned it "After Hours Fraternizing." The second and third pictures are of Carter and me in my rental car parked in front of the hotel. Whoever took the photo must've done so from the lobby. The shots are pretty creative. In both, I'm leaning across Carter's seat to tell the valet that I'm checking out, but the photos make it appear as if she and I are kissing. The two photos are captioned, "Caught in the Act." There's no return address, only a note that threatens to expose me as a philandering CEO if I don't leave Carter alone. The sender is giving me five days to comply. It doesn't take a brain surgeon to figure out who's behind all of this.

I dial Grace. I tap my fingers against the desk, waiting for her to answer. The call goes to voicemail.

"What a way to get my attention. You want your meeting? Let's have one. 558 Leaf Court Drive. Be there at eight o'clock Tuesday morning."

I feel like throwing the phone at the wall after I hang up. I fucked up big-time. Carter should not be here. I weigh wanting to fuck her against the need to redefine myself. One greatly outweighs the other.

As soon as I stand, my cell phone chimes with a new message. I pick it up and look at the screen.

The message is from Grace, and it simply says, "K."
I sniff disdainfully. I haven't known her to be so
casual about the vile shit she does. She'll never have
a thing to do with Kennedy Creative once I get
done with her.

I feel as if I'm in complete control of my libido
when I make it back out to the pool. Despite her
earlier trepidation, Carter has made herself
comfortable in the warm water. She's wearing a
white bathing suit and swim cap. I watch her swim
a lap, and when she touches the wall, she wipes the
water out of her eyes and looks at me with a smile.

"Is it warm?" I ask.

"Nice and toasty. It sure did warm up fast."

I walk over to her and squat at the pool edge. "I
had an eighty-thousand-dollar heating system
installed."

She snickers. "Rich people's solutions."

I wink. "And now you get to swim in a rich
man's pool."

I can tell by the look in her eyes that she wants
to do more than swim in my pool. She wants my
dick to swim inside her hot pool of sweetness. The
temptation to fuck her is back with a vengeance—
especially since the pussy is warmer after a woman
takes a swim.

"What are you thinking?" she asks.

I've learned that Carter is pretty perceptive. I stand. "I'm thinking I'd better get into the pool or you're going to use all the warm water."

She smiles weakly. "That's not what you were thinking."

I grin flirtatiously. "Not all of it, but I do want to hurry up and join you."

Carter lets go of the edge and treads water. "And then you'll tell me all of it?"

I head to the men's changing room. "We'll talk!"

"I can't wait!"

I hear her beating the water as she swims before I enter the changing room. I take off my clothes, put on a pair of swimming trunks, and go dive into the pool. The warm water is refreshing. Carter's in the middle of another lap. I swim a lap, passing her at a safe distance. I make it to the end of the pool before she does. Since she's breathing heavily and has been at it longer than I have, I swim toward her. Surprisingly, she passes me again. When I make it to the spot she just left, Carter's already holding on to the edge. She's breathing heavily but smiling victoriously.

I laugh. "Are you that competitive?"

She shrugs coyly while breathing heavily. "I can't help myself when it comes to you. Meet me in the middle?"

"Is this a trick?" I ask.

"No," she says flirtatiously.

I take her at her word and swim to the middle of the pool. We arrive at the same time and tread water.

"You like playing games?" I ask.

She's still grinning. "Not really."

"So what have I done to put you in such a playful mood?"

She dips into the water then comes back up. "It's what you haven't done." Her hand squeezes my dick.

I feel the blood drain from my face. My dick is growing, so I remove the culprit. "I can't."

She flexes her eyebrows. "Why not?"

I must admit that up until this very moment, I was confused about how I saw Carter. She definitely has the figure of a woman, including squeezable tits and ass. I admire that she's a damn good architect. I credit her proficiency to natural talent, but I've seen her read design and architecture books as if they were novels, which means she's well studied. I can see why guys like Tyler, Matt, and a half a dozen other men in the company grow boners whenever she walks into the room. She walks her hot ass into the building every morning, paying no one any mind, sits in her chair, and gets right to work. That ritual of hers makes her mysterious. Right now, she's a beautiful young woman who's not used to waiting so long for a guy to pounce on her.

"You're my employee," I say.

"I knew you long before I became your employee."

Shit. I have to remind myself of what's important here. I sink into the water and come back up. It's way too warm to cool my lust.

I dip my head toward the edge of the pool. "Follow me."

I don't have to guess whether or not she obeys. I climb out of the swimming pool, and Carter's right behind me. I sit on one of the long chairs, and she sits beside me. I let my dick inform on me. It's hard and long, and she can't take her eyes off my rod.

"As you can see, I want you bad."

Carter shoots to her feet. "Then take me."

She steps out of her wet bathing suit. I'm mesmerized by her nakedness.

I take her by the hand. "I'm flattered that you want to give yourself to me."

"But…"

"Just sit."

She picks her bathing suit up off the ground and uses the wet garment to cover herself.

I push the suit down so that I can see her body. "Don't be ashamed. I want you. Why wouldn't I? You're hot." I take a long sigh. "But, Carter, I have fucking issues. If I fuck you, I don't know what will happen to me."

She frowns. "You're not making any sense."

"You know those rumors you heard about me before I came on board?"

She shrugs. I take that as a yes.

"They're true. I fucked more than half of the women in my other company. And do you know why Vince doesn't talk to me anymore?"

She shakes her head.

"His girlfriend worked for our company, and eventually I fucked her too."

"Oh." She finally has a reaction to something I said. "Well, that explains it."

"Explains what?"

"Allie has been trying to figure out why Vince broke up with his girlfriend and started dating that model."

Now I'm the one who's taken aback. "What model?"

Carter snaps her fingers as she tries to recall the name. "Oh, it's Cindy O'Lay."

"Vince is dating her?" I sound more disgusted than I am. I'm just surprised. I never thought he'd leave Maggie for anyone, not even Cleopatra resurrected from the dead.

"Yes. Allie, Maddie, and Lexie…" Carter ruffles her eyebrows. "Those names make them sound like the queens of the WASPs that they are."

I chuckle. "They are the queens of the WASPs."

She grins appreciatively. "They hated Vince's girlfriend, but they hate Cindy O'Lay even more. I think it's because she has more hair and is skinnier than they are."

I laugh, but it's not enough to take the stiff out of my dick.

Carter shakes her head and rolls her eyes. The thought of her cousins has put her in a cynical mood. "I heard they tried to pawn him off on Emily Callahan of all people."

I lift a finger. "I fucked her too."

Her eyes widen. "No fucking way."

"I bet you don't want to fuck the same guy who

fucked his way through all of Vince's girlfriends and half of his female employees."

Carter drops her swimsuit back on the ground and gets comfortable in her chair. "Well, now that you put it like that…"

She's joking, but I can tell by her demeanor that I finally got through to her.

"I have one thing in this fucking world that I want right now."

She looks me square in the eyes. "What's that?"

"I want Vince to forgive me, but I need more than his forgiveness. I need him to trust me, and I need to know he can trust me."

We stare into each other's eyes. Finally I can articulate what I've been feeling ever since Vince decided to have nothing more to do with me. Carter holds out her hand. I put my hand on top of hers. Our fingers curl around each other's, and we sit in silence for a long time.

"Robert, are you still asleep?" Carter says.

I'm groggy, but I can focus on her pretty face. "No."

She checks her watch. "We must've fallen asleep two hours ago."

"We had an eventful morning." I'm mostly

referring to those fucking pictures Grace dropped on my porch.

"Well…" Carter stands. She's still naked, and my dick springs back to life. "A few laps should wake me up." She dives into the pool.

I watch her swim from one end of the pool to the other. She swims four laps then clings to the edge to catch her breath.

"You're in great shape," I say.

She pushes herself out of the water and sits on the edge. "I used to compete in high school. The old girl isn't what she used to be."

I laugh. "You're only twenty-five."

"Who said I was twenty-five?"

"You alluded to it."

"No, *you* alluded to it. I never confirmed or denied it." She shakes her head. "I'll always be younger than what I really am to you. But just so you can stop guessing, I'm twenty-six."

I smile at her. There's no need to point out that there isn't much of a difference between twenty-five and twenty-six. I join her for some laps. I fool around and push her in the pool, then she pushes me. I'm having a good time dunking her head in the water. She wraps me up around the waist and tries to pull me underwater.

Suddenly, I lose my head and guide her in front of me. Before I know it, I have her pinned against the edge of the swimming pool. My tongue is in her mouth, and my dick is rubbing against her pussy.

I pull my mouth off hers. "Shit. No." My heart is beating a mile a minute.

Carter holds me tighter. "Robert, if you bang it, you don't have to buy it."

It takes a second for me to understand what she means by that. Basically, if I fuck her, then it doesn't have to be the start of some great and meaningful relationship. I just remember how sweet her mouth tasted and how soft her lips were. I kiss her again. My dick begs me to let him inside her pussy.

I drop my face to end the kiss. "I've done enough banging without buying."

She's breathing heavily while pelting my forehead and cheeks with kisses. I'm used to women being hot for me to fuck them once I get them to this point. This entire situation is my fucking fault. I call on help from my intuition. Suddenly I hear Maggie say, "Robert is a lost soul only because Vince has done a mighty fine job of enabling him."

I take Carter's hand off my dick. "We can't."

She frowns then pulls away from me. "Okay." Her voice cracks.

"Listen…" I say.

She swims to the opposite side of the pool, and I swim after her. Carter makes it to the steps. I grab hold of her before she can take both feet out of the pool. Her body is so soft and cool, which means her insides are warm. I just want to plunge into her hot depths.

"It's okay," she says. "I'll get over it."

I spin her around. We lock eyes. I make a split-second decision and kiss her sweet mouth. Our tongues roll round each other. Her hard nipples poke my chest. I'm so hard that I'm going to explode.

"Shit," I mutter and lift her all the way off the steps and carry her to solid ground.

Then I lift her legs up and around my waist. Carter's moaning and whimpering. I've never been with a woman this eager. She sucks the skin of my neck between her teeth. It feels so damn sensual. There's no way we'll make it back to the house, so I carry her into the men's changing room. Carter sucks on my nipples as I lay her on the massage bed. My dick is so hard that it's plastered against my stomach. I pull down my swimming trunks.

Carter's eyes grow wide at the sight of my fat dick. "Shit, you're huge."

She sits up, wraps her warm and clammy hand around my cock, and shifts it up and down. I close my eyes to feel the blood flood my shaft. Then a wet, warm mouth surrounds it. I make the mistake of looking down to see her mouth fuck my dick. I quickly shut my eyes and concentrate on not coming.

"Enough," I whisper and guide her back onto the massage bed.

It's my turn to taste her. I cover her clit with my mouth and suck and lick. Her creamy juices moisten my face, and as soon as she comes, I intend to lick and taste it all.

Carter screams and says, "Oh shit!"

She tries to lift her head, but she quickly pins it back down to the bed. I want her to come harder than she ever has, so I stop working the front of the clit and guide my tongue to the side of her clit. Carter moans and sucks air. She doesn't sound like a porn star, and I'm satisfied. That's a classic sign that a woman is faking it. I keep my eyes on her tits. I can't wait to bite those nipples. Suddenly she screams and shivers. I slow my tongue motion to make her orgasm last.

"Oh, Robert, oh, Robert, oh, Robert…" she whimpers as I consume her juices.

I tell myself that I can stop now and not fall deeper into the shit I've just stepped in, but instead I spread her legs, crawl between them, and let my cock have what he's been craving.

Carter's pussy is hot and wet. My dick thanks me for letting it slide in and out of her deliciousness. I stroke her nice and slow so that she can feel all ten inches of my fat dick rub against her nerves. The slippery friction makes me want to release prematurely. My rule is to never come before she comes. Even though I feel an enormous amount of guilt for fucking her, I can't get lazy. I make women come and not with just my mouth. Carter screeches and holds on tighter.

"Lift your hips, baby," I say.

After a moment, she follows my instruction. I work the inside of her pussy until I discover her most sensitive spot.

"Do you feel that?"

"Yes!"

I put my hands under her ass to keep her stable. Carter's screaming some indiscernible shit. Her fingernails claw my back. She may have broken skin as she shrieks so loud that her voice echoes throughout the room. Now that she's come, I fuck her harder and deeper until I'm ready to blow. I pull out and shoot my load all over her belly.

Now that we've started, we can't stop. We kiss all the way back to my bedroom, where I fuck her some more. This time, I wear a condom. There's no way I'm ready to bring offspring into the world. We forgo food so that she can blow me until I blow her. I eat her clit and finger fuck her until she squirts.

And now we lie side by side, looking at the ceiling.

"How do you feel?" she asks.

I close my eyes. No woman's ever asked me that question after I gave it to her so good. The truth is that I feel like a fucking failure. All I had to do was keep my dick and my tongue out of her pussy.

"That bad?" she says.

"No, I'm fine." My tone is coarse.

She turns on her side and faces away from me. "Like I said, just because you banged it doesn't mean you have to buy it."

I lie on my side and spoon her. "I heard you, but I wanted to buy the next woman I banged." I chuckle.

"That's a tall order for a modern man."

I reach around to play with her nipple. I've

eaten the shit out of her tits, so they should still be nice and tender.

Carter sucks air. "You're the best, Robert Tango."

I'm too confused about how I feel to say thank you.

"I've wanted to fuck you just about all my life," she says. "So really, don't blame yourself for what we've done. I wasn't going to leave here until you gave me what I wanted."

I chuckle. "Glad to hear that I was the one being seduced."

Carter sighs. "You *definitely* were."

I turn her on her back, and we kiss until I rise again. This time we make serious love. I fucking feel like crying because her pussy feels so good. Not only that, but my soul wants to merge with hers. But fuck, she's only twenty-six years old. What does a twenty-six-year-old woman really know about the world? I can't fall in love with Carter long-term, but I can let myself fall in love with her at this moment. I thrust inside her, caress her, and kiss and bite her neck. She squeezes me tightly and shoves her hip against my cock so that I go deeper. When I come, I hold her so tightly that I'm afraid I might break her. *Or she may break me.*

❄

CARTER AND I CLEAN UP, get dressed, and drive downtown for dinner at a bistro on Jefferson Street. The waitress takes our order, smiles, and says she'll get it to us soon.

Carter rolls her eyes. "I guess I'm invisible."

I frown.

"Don't tell me you didn't notice all the service she was giving you?" She sees my even more confused expression and leans across the table. "Oh, don't look at me as if I'm a psycho jealous lover. That chick totally ignored me."

I laugh because that thought was slowly coming to mind.

"Anyway, you're obviously beautiful, sexy, and good in bed, so what's a girl to do but try to make you her own?" she says.

I smile as I bask in her beauty. "Have you always been this funny?"

She winks. "Yes."

I laugh.

"But just so you know, if lightning struck me dead, then I would die perfectly content," she says.

"And why is that?"

"You did me."

I sniff a chuckle. I want to be serious about all the sex we just had. A large part of me wants to buy the pussy I just banged, but am I ready for a full-on relationship? "Why did you say that if I bang it, then I don't have to buy it?"

Carter does her customary eye roll. "Because where you're from, a woman only rations out the pussy as an investment."

"Where I'm from?"

"I've dated Middle-America-minded boys before. One fuck, and they think I want to marry them at some point. That's not where I'm from."

"Me neither," I say.

She picks up her glass of water. "Robert Tango, you've made yourself a man of the world for sure, but your issues—you know, the ones that fueled the rumors?—they stem from you trying to disassociate yourself from the rigid shit someone tried to shove down your throat during your formative years. I mean, that's exactly what's wrong with Maddie, Allie, and Lexie. They all married the first man they fucked after the age of twenty-one."

I take a moment to contemplate everything she just said. I realize that she's mixing humor with social theories. This isn't the first time I've sat with someone who tried to figure out what's wrong with most people in our society, but they're usually stoned.

"Have you been smoking marijuana?" I ask.

She tosses her head back to laugh. "I partake in the exotic bush every now and then, but not at the moment." She waves flippantly. "Just forget everything I just said. You didn't ask me to play your shrink."

I shake my head. "No, it's okay. Speak your mind. You've certainly come alive tonight."

"That's because I have nothing to lose."

I furrow my eyebrows, wondering what she means by that. I'm about to ask when the waitress brings my whisky and Carter's cherry martini.

The waitress smiles only at me. "Enjoy."

Carter pats her arm. "Excuse me?"

She turns her smile toward Carter.

"Do you want me to enjoy this drink as well?"

At first the waitress ruffles her eyebrows as if she's confused, but then she snorts. "Yeah, right. Sorry, he's hot."

That breaks the ice, because the two women share a good laugh at the expense of my "hotness." The waitress gives me one more lustful look as she walks away.

I put my focus back on Carter. "Hey, what did you mean by you had nothing to lose?"

She shakes her head passively. "Forget it."

I feel as if she's hiding something from me, but I choose to respect her wishes. Our dinner comes, and we reminisce about Vince and his sisters. Carter also has a lot of questions about my marriage to Lena. Where did we meet? How did I feel when I first saw her? I'm forced to speak the truth.

"The sad truth is I wanted her because Vince wanted her. I went too far when I married her." I feel like shit again. "I've been the worst buddy he could have for most of our lives."

Carter frowns as she balks. "I'm not big on easing self-pity, but I can honestly say that that's not true."

"No?"

"You were the brother that Vince needed. Um, Maddie, Allie, and Lexi… hello…"

I laugh.

"I love them, but they're the witches of Eastwick. If it weren't for you, Vince would be wearing Easter-egg yellow golfing khakis and a Polo shirt with black-and-white Oxfords. He'd be married to the queen of the Stepford wives with three little objects they parade around on Sunday mornings to show the world they've gotten with the program. You made Vince edgy, and he should thank his lucky stars for that."

I study her expression. She really believes what she just said, but I'm not sure if I do. "I thought you were close to Allie, Maddie, and Lexie?"

She nods with her trademark eye roll. "We are."

I can't help but laugh. "You sound as if you regret it."

"They're always on my ass. Allie has called three times since I've been here. And Maddie called because Allie couldn't get in touch with me." She raises a finger pointedly. "Oh, and then Allie called Tyler to ask if I was with him."

I feel my whole face frown. "Tyler?"

"He called me to ask where I am."

I flinch, taken aback. "And did you tell him?"

She gazes off thoughtfully. "No, I didn't."

I study her as she remains in her thoughts for a moment. I've seen that look on a woman's face before. I may have fucked another woman who's still in love with another man.

Our food arrives, and we get through the rest of dinner by sharing our dream projects. Once we're done with our meal, I pay the bill, and we return to my place. I ask Carter if she would like to sleep in a freshly made bed for the night, but she prefers to stay in the room that I originally offered her. And now we're standing face-to-face. Although I suspect she's in love with the douchebag that threw her out of her own apartment, my dick wants to go another round with her pussy. Why not? She's a woman. I'm a man. And that's a bed.

I kiss her forehead and step away from her. "Have a good night's sleep."

Carter nods as if she understands the decision I just made. "You too."

I walk out of the room and close the door. It's late, but to get my lust under control, I decide to go for a run. I haven't exercised in so long that I can't say when my last workout was. I put on a pair of sweats, a long sleeved T-shirt, and my running shoes and head out into the night. The course that I run in Napa looks better in the daytime. All the homes in my neighborhood are set far away from the road, so I'm mostly jogging past fields of grape vines, tall and skinny Italian spruce trees, and trimmed shrubs. The farther out of my neighborhood I jog, the darker it gets. I hear my breath, my footsteps, and the wind whistling past my ear.

I think about what Carter said. If it weren't for

me, Vince would be a different kind of man. I'm well aware that if it weren't for him and his family, I would be a different kind of man. About eleven years ago, Vince convinced me to invest my trust fund in high-yielding stocks. As a result, I more than quadrupled my investment, and so did he. That's when we pooled our money, found another investor, and started our media company. I now believe that I do deserve some credit for making A&Rt Media the success that it is. When we first started, I was the one who studied corporate structures. I put together the pieces and formed the right departments to accelerate our growth. I hired the employees. Gabe Zenith was actually my first. After our first year of operation, we were less than a million dollars in the red. After our second year of operating, we were 375 million in the black. I can only half kick myself for not letting Vince buy me out then. I had taken my talents as far as I could within the industry of media. However, if I had left then, I may still have Vince as my best buddy, but I wouldn't be 2.3 billion dollars richer. And maybe I wouldn't have Vince as my best buddy. I would've eventually done something to fuck up our friendship.

Without realizing it, I increased my pace from a

jog to a sprint. I stop and bend over, grabbing my knees to catch my breath. Maybe I'm willing to do right by Carter. I had a good time connecting with her sexually today. At some points, I sort of felt as if we were making love. Just being close to her filled my heart with a sensation that I've never felt before. I believe that I'm ready to give a normal relationship a try.

It's pitch black out here. I didn't wear my watch, but I have to have been running for the last forty-five minutes or so. My first inclination is to walk at least the first mile and a half back then jog the rest. I've already overexerted myself. But Carter is at the house. I can't wait to tell her that I want to give "us" a chance and make love to her throughout the rest of the night. So I jog all the way back home and increase my pace as I go. Approximately a half an hour later, I arrive at the front porch. I want to bend over to catch my breath, but I can do that after I'm in Carter's room.

"Carter," I call as I run down the steps to her bedroom.

She doesn't answer, so I knock on the door and wait. I'm breathing heavily. She doesn't answer, so I knock again. I wait a few beats. Still there's no answer.

I open the door slowly. "Carter?"

I take three steps into the bedroom and stop. Her luggage and bags of stuff aren't lined up against the wall. The bed is made, and the bathroom light is off. Shit, I don't have to be a rocket scientist to figure out she's gone—but how in the hell did she get out of here without a car? Someone must've picked her up.

11

THE AMAZING DISAPPEARING ACT

CARTER

AN HOUR AGO...

*C*arter couldn't sleep even if she tried to force herself to do it. She sat on the bed, listening for any sign that Robert had changed his mind and decided to join her. She sat at attention when she heard his bedroom door open and his footsteps. She ascertained that he was walking up the stairs and not toward her room. Then she scrambled out of bed to look out the window and saw him jogging down the long driveway. She stood there watching him until the night had claimed him. Carter wondered what to do next. Her body yearned for more of Robert Tango, but she was also confused about Tyler. She believed him when he said that he hadn't asked the landlord to put her out of the apartment. But if he didn't do it, then who did?

Since Robert had gone for a run, Carter lurked through the house. He had given her a tour earlier, but she preferred to indulge in these things alone. So far the floor plan was just as she would have drawn it. She had her cell phone with her to take pictures of some of the walls. Robert had used some great plasters and wall glass throughout the house. She was a few minutes into her self-guided tour and had just entered Robert's home office when she received a call. Carter checked the name on the screen. It was Tyler.

She sighed before answering. "Hello?"

"Hi."

Carter noted the height of the walls, then she saw the envelope Robert had earlier sitting on the desk. "It's late. What do you want?" she said, half distracted.

"I just wanted to talk to you."

For one second, she debated whether or not she should invade Robert's privacy. She was good at keeping things to herself, so he would never find out that she had snooped. If only he hadn't behaved so strangely after he had returned to the garage, darn near clinging to that envelope.

"Where are you?" Tyler asked.

Carter held still for moment to make sure she couldn't hear Robert returning from his run. After a beat, she felt as if the coast was clear. "In Napa."

"Me too," Tyler said excitedly.

She rolled her eyes as she slid the contents out of the envelope. "No, you're not." Carter gasped at the photos of her and Robert.

"What's going on?" Tyler asked.

She read the note attached, threatening Robert if he didn't fire her. "Did you send Robert pictures of him and I together, threatening him to leave me alone or else?"

"Picture? Is that who you're with, Tango?"

"Fuck." Carter knew she had said too much. "Yes. But that's not what I asked."

"Are you two fucking?"

It was time to lie. "No. He and I are friends from childhood."

"No way. Are you dicking me around?"

"No, it's true."

He grunted, sounding intrigued. "No wonder."

"No, no wonder," she snapped. "I earned my shit, and you know it."

Tyler remained quiet as Carter slid the photos back into the envelope. She was more conflicted now than she had been before she began the tour. If there was one thing she'd learned by spending the day with the man she'd crushed on her whole life, it was that he needed an unsullied reputation.

Carter tried her best to place the envelope just as she found it. "Are you really in Napa?"

"Yes," he said.

She closed her eyes to consider whether or not she was being impulsive with her next decision. At the moment, everything she had questioned was clear. Although her heart already felt the loss of Robert Tango making love to her once again, she sighed with resolve. "Could you come pick me up?"

Tyler didn't hesitate. "What's the address?"

ROBERT

This is the fifth time I've tried to call Carter since she disappeared in the middle of the night. I left a message on the first call, asking her to call me back and let me know that she hadn't been abducted by aliens. She'd left pretty abruptly, so I can only guess that something's gone wrong. Her voicemail picks up again.

"I get your message loud and clear. At least text me to tell me that you're okay and that I don't have to worry." I end the call. I would never admit this out loud, but I'm hurt. More than likely, it's just a shot to my ego and a smidgen to my heart.

It's Sunday afternoon. Today the transport company brought my vehicle over and took my rental car back to the company. It feels good to sit in the driver's seat of my own car again. I had them bring my brand new sporty Jaguar. I'm heading back to San Francisco to stay in Jack's Russian Hill house. I'm tempted to call Grace and ask her to meet me for drinks tonight. I want to get to the bottom of those photos. It's driving me crazy that she paid someone to take those pictures in order to get some leverage over me. However, I'm too preoccupied by what could've possibly happened to Carter to even deal with Grace right now. I decide to keep our original meeting time of Tuesday morning at eight.

It's already nighttime when I make it to Jack's house. The lights are on inside. He directed me to just ring the doorbell, and one of the "house staff" would let me in. I barely get Jack Lord. For a pretty down-to-earth guy, he has some fucking stuffy habits. He has personal chefs and daily caretakers in all the homes he owns. He owns eight houses that I know of, and that doesn't include his three private islands. He's just a man with too much fucking money. Thank goodness that his heart is made of the finest quality of gold.

His Russian Hill house is an extravagant Victorian complete with two limestone lion statues at the foot of the tall steps. I drive past the front of the house and turn down a narrow driveway. I'm supposed to drive all the way to a closed two-car garage, park my car, walk through a gate, and ring the doorbell of the first door that I see. I follow those instructions to a T. There's not a drop of light back here, and I'm a little worried until the porch light cuts on. Less than a minute later, a tiny black woman opens the door. She might be fifty or sixty, I don't know, but her enthusiasm is inviting.

"Hello, darling," she says with a Caribbean accent.

"Good evening."

She looks over her shoulder. "Clarence, come get the man's luggage."

An older white man, who looks to be in his early

sixties, shoots past me and stops behind me. "Car keys?"

I hesitate, but I give him my keys.

"I'll park it in the garage and bring your suitcases up," he says.

Clarence is frail. I'm twice his height and size.

"That's okay, I can get my suitcases," I say.

"No, no," the black lady says. "I know you're a big, strong man, but Clarence is too, aren't you, darling?"

Clarence simpers and goes off to do his job.

I raise my eyebrows. They're a couple.

"Come on in and eat dinner," she says.

I can smell the spicy food coming from the house. Hell, she doesn't have to tell me twice to come and eat.

"My name is Mary, and that's my husband, Clarence," she says as I follow her.

She tells me where I'll be sleeping and who will be here in the morning to cook breakfast.

"I cook in the night and clean in the day," she says.

I'm trying to follow her every word, but I'm awed by the inside of the house. Like Jack Lord himself, the house is a contradiction. The outside looks old and traditional, but the inside is a modern masterpiece. He's had the house gutted from top to bottom and put in clean and modern fixtures, flooring, staircases, fireplaces, and furnishings throughout. Even the floor plan has been modernized. Anyone in his or her right mind would advise Jack against doing what he did—he completely gutted the house's worth. However, it's not as if he needs to think about resale value. Instead, what he has here is a masterpiece, and I half want to ask him if he would sell the damn house to me!

It seems Jack is partial to sunroom dining areas where the walls are made of glass and it seems as if we're eating outside. He has the same kind of room in his Malibu beach house and his Manhattan apartment. I'm sitting at the dining room table, and a lit garden surrounds the glass encasement. I would have loved to bring Carter back to this house. She could really appreciate what Jack has done.

My cell phone vibrates. I take it out of my pants pocket. Speak of the angel, I just received a text from Carter. It says, "I'm fine. Sorry for the sudden departure. I had fun. I wish you the best."

I stare at the words. "I wish you the best." That sounds so final. I have a good mind to call her back, but I think better of it. Shit, what a spot I'm in. I remember Zoe's warning about losing respect if I fucked Carter. She didn't come out and say it, but I got the gist of her words. Yes, it's best to deal with Carter another day.

Mary serves me beef stroganoff and a fresh pepper salad. The food is good, and I scarf down two helpings before heading upstairs to bed. I've had a long, mentally draining day. The guest room is fit for a king and puts all four of my guest rooms to shame. I feel as if I'm staying in a five-star hotel with a flat king-sized bed that has a backboard coated with onyx. There's an egg-shaped tub that sits on a dark wood plank. A bubble bath has already been drawn for me. The light fixtures are metalwork nightstand lamps carved into inter-secting circles surrounding a ball of pleasant light. A fluffy white fur rug surrounds the bed. I definitely have to up my design game to outdo Jack Lord's house.

I strip out of my clothes and get into the tub. The water is so comfortable that I almost drift off to sleep. I get out, dry off, and hit the sack. I lay in the dark for a while, trying to figure out how in the hell I'll handle these feelings I have for a woman who's off-limits and way too young for my tastes. However, Carter isn't immature.

Am I ready to be in something serious? I feel

like an open wound that's in the healing stage. Nothing in my life can be good as long as Vince wants nothing to do with me. No. I need to make this business successful, and I'll show him that I've changed. Only then will I be ready to be involved with the right woman.

I turn on my side and close my eyes. "Shit."

The first thought that comes to my head is a memory of sucking on Carter's ripe nipples. I grab my dick, let my memory replay more scenes of us fucking, and take care of myself.

MONDAY MORNING ARRIVES. This is officially the first morning that I've slept in. It's ten o'clock, and I needed every ounce of the extra sleep. I contact Pierce Daly, the broker Jack told me to get in touch with, and I tell him that I'm interested in at least three acres of land so that I can build the Robert Tango brand of a mid-century modern style estate. Pierce tells me three acres in the city is hard to find but not impossible.

"I'd like to see something today," I say.

He hesitates. "I'll call you back in a couple of hours."

"That's what I like to hear," I say. A good real estate broker will rise to the occasion.

I scoot to the foot of the bed and notice a small white card in front of the closed door. I go pick it up. It says to dial the intercom when I'm ready for breakfast, so that's exactly what I do. The cook agrees to bring breakfast upstairs.

I still have a lot of work details on my mind. Despite being on a four-day weekend, I'm receiving emails left and right about every facet of my business. I fight the urge to go to the office, set up my computer, and work for the rest of the day. Instead, I turn on the television, click the On Demand button, and veg out on TV shows as I eat breakfast.

Two hours after I finish eating, I receive a call from Pierce. He has four plots to show me today. I put on a pair of jeans and a sweater and ring the intercom to let Clarence know that I'll need my car. He tells me it'll be ready in five minutes.

Shit, no wonder Jack lives like this. One phone call, and everything I need is at my fingertips. It's like having personal house elves. It's plain insane. Living like this makes me feel lazy, but I only have to put up with it until I finish building my own place.

Later in the day, I choose the third plot Pierce

shows me. It's on the west end the city, on a hilltop in Sea Cliff where I can have three-hundred-sixty-degree views of the beach, downtown, and the Golden Gate Bridge. On the drive home, I realize that I'm Zen. My soul has never felt so satisfied. I'm doing this. I'm changing my life. I grin Zoe style. Life has never been so good.

12

TWO CRAZIES IN A COMPANY

TUESDAY MORNING...

'm working in Jack's study. Grace walks in and stops as if she's caught off guard by the ambiance. I let her have a moment to admire the white cabinets with checkered white-and-clear glass doors behind my desk.

"Interesting house you have here," she says.

I do believe that was a compliment, although her deadpan tone doesn't indicate one. I point at the white leather chair across from my desk. "Have a seat."

Grace studies me with ruffled eyebrows as she sits. "I didn't come here to fight."

I place the envelope of photos in front of her. "Do you recognize that?"

She tilts her head curiously. "Should I?"

"Open it."

Grace hesitates but opens the envelope, takes the pictures out, and studies them. She scoffs. "You don't think I did this, do you?"

I sit back confidently in my chair. "I do."

"I'm not saying that this is beneath me, but I didn't do it."

"I'm sure you weren't the photographer, but you're behind this shit."

Grace remains as cool as a cucumber as she watches me with an unaffected grin. "So you've been fucking Carter. Great."

I point at the pictures. "Those photos are doctored."

She looks off and shakes her head. "That bitch never ceases to amaze me. But as I said, I'm not behind this."

For the short time that I've known Grace, I've learned that lying isn't her MO. She would cop to the truth at some point—and now would be that time.

I sigh. "I believe you, but if you didn't send this, then I wonder who did."

Grace picks up the photos of Carter and me in the car. She grimaces as she studies them. "You were staying at the St. Regis?"

"I'm sure you knew that already."

"It's not a secret. Everybody knows you were staying there," she says, distracted by a photo that she turns this way and that. "This picture looks as if it was taken from the lobby." She puts down the photo. "You bring me back into the fold effective immediately, and I'll help you find whoever did this."

I study her with one eye narrowed. I've been asked by a number of people if I'll hire Grace on full-time now that her three months are up. My answer has been an unwavering no. I think about the idea I had in mind for her, but I wasn't planning on presenting the offer until she had at least six months of psychotherapy under her belt. However, it's mighty superior of me to presume that she needs a shrink. And that's what I feel at the moment —that I'm being a fucking superior prick.

"Only if you can prove that you really didn't put those pictures on my doorstep."

"I told you I didn't."

"Also, I can't bring you back in on the architecture side. You've burned all of your fucking bridges there."

She snorts sharply. "No, I have not."

Grace can so easily make her pretty face ugly. I

believe making her face ugly like that is a way to knock her opponent off center.

"Oh yes, you have," I say, sticking to my guns.

She rolls her eyes.

I raise a finger. "Don't say another word, because I don't want you to make me change my mind." I wait. She remains silent. Good. "As you know, I'm changing the name of my company."

Grace squirms. I can tell she hates the sound of that.

"However, I'm keeping Kennedy Creative as a subsidiary of RT Modern Design."

She scoffs.

I raise a finger to signal her to allow me to continue. "Kennedy Creative will be our interior design studio, and I was hoping you could run that arm."

The scowl on her face slowly fades to shock.

"Is it a deal?" I ask.

She clears her throat and swallows. "It's a deal."

I extend my hand so that we can shake on it. Grace's palms are dewy, and she's shaking a little. "Good."

She sniffs as she takes her hand back and regains her superior posture. "Well, I guess I'll make that call."

I narrow an eye. "What call?"

Grace takes her cell phone out of her purse and riffles through her contact list. "Just tell me what time and date these photos were taken. I know someone who can pull the footage from the cameras in the hotel lobby."

GRACE'S CONTACT asked when she needed to see the footage, and she said, "Two days ago." He said to give him an hour. The video shouldn't be hard to obtain since it was only four nights ago.

That was thirty minutes ago. Now I'm driving to the hotel, and Grace is riding shotgun. She wanted to drive, but I told her that it's time she gets used to me being in charge of her. That got a chuckle out of her. When I look at her, it's as though a dark veil has been lifted from over her face. Deep down, I knew that if I gave Grace her own design arm to run, it would probably rid her of a tiny bit of the bitterness she harbors.

"I have to ask," she says. "What were you doing alone with Carter?"

We've been riding in silence for the last ten minutes, and I kind of liked it that way. I could tell she had something to say, and I guessed Carter would be the topic of discussion.

"I was giving her a ride," I say.

"A ride home?"

I clench my jaw. "Yes."

She goes silent. I hope that's the end of questions about Carter.

"I don't believe it," she says. "I don't understand what men see in her. She's so… blah."

Good sense tells me to not reply. I know that Grace is baiting me. She wants to know why *I* like Carter so much.

"Yes, she has that tight little body and those pretty eyes, but no spark, no fire," she says.

"What the hell is spark and fire?" I ask, hating that I let her lure me into this discussion.

"She has a blank look on her face all the time. She's not that attractive."

I snort.

"Oh, you think she's attractive?" she asks.

I feel as if that question is merely a trick. I think she can sense that something happened between Carter and me, and she's trying to chisel her way to the truth. But one thing I've always been good at is getting someone off my ass.

"I've known Carter for thirteen, fourteen years," I say.

She watches me with narrowed eyes. "What?"

"She's my best friend's cousin. I used to spend summers with her and her family in Sag Harbor."

Grace gazes out the window. We're stopped at a light.

"She's like part of the family." I'm exaggerating, but I don't give a damn. Whatever it takes to keep Grace off my ass about Carter.

"But why didn't you say anything before?"

"It's nobody's business."

"Robert, what you do with your employees is everybody's business. Why do you think those photos have so much influence?"

The light turns green, and I go. "Because I've been fucking up for a while and developed a reputation."

I'm waiting for Grace's response, but she's silent. I turn down the same street of the hotel.

"Well, you haven't fucked up my father's company, and for that, I appreciate you. And photos like that can take down the most straitlaced CEOs."

I turn to look at her in shock. Damn, she just gave me a compliment.

Grace grabs the dashboard. "Watch it!"

I quickly face the road. "Shit!" I jam on my brakes and narrowly avoid colliding with a car that's stopped in front of me. I check my rearview mirror. Thankfully no one was behind me.

I put a hand on Grace's arm. "Are you all right?"

She's staring at my hand. I remove it.

"Yes," she says. "Could you just keep your eyes on the road?"

"Yes, I can. You just shocked the hell out of me with your compliment."

"Well, I won't give those to you anymore, at least not while you're driving."

I think she just told a joke. I glance at her. She's half smiling. That *was* a joke.

WE MAKE it to the hotel, and Grace's contact meets us in the lobby. He's a young guy in his twenties, wearing a suit with a security logo on the jacket. His name is Brent, and Brent and Grace grin at each other. Speaking of two people who look as if they've fucked before... I keep my thoughts to myself as he and I shake hands, and he leads us to the control room.

"What you were looking for wasn't hard to find. This guy isn't a professional," Brent says.

"It's a guy?" I ask.

Grace elbows me gently. "I told you I didn't do it."

"He thought it was you?" Brent says as if he can't believe Grace would ever do something like that.

"That's because he doesn't know me like you do," she says to Brent then winks at me.

I shake my head. I'm sort of charmed by her, which surprises the shit out of me.

Once we get to the control room, all the monitors are on and the video is cued up. Brent tells us that he had to pull some strings to let us into this room. I'm sure he's hoping that it will win him some fuck points with Grace.

Grace rubs his back. "That's what you do—the impossible."

I stop myself from blowing sharply between my teeth. Poor guy, she's playing him.

Brent turns red. He cuts on the video and puts his finger on the screen. "And there he goes."

Grace and I move in closer to the screen. Our

faces almost collide, and we both draw back a smidgen.

"Well, well, well…" Grace says, grimacing.

"Well, well, well indeed," I say.

"So what are you going to do, Robert?"

"There's only one thing to do."

Grace is still staring at the culprit with the camera as though she has a lot on her mind.

"Thanks for showing this to me," I say to Brent and pass him five one-hundred-dollar bills.

He flinches, taken aback. "Anytime." He's a happy camper.

"Ready?" I ask Grace.

She's still lost in the video. "Huh?"

"I asked if you're ready."

She tears her eyes off the screen. "Sure, right."

Grace hugs Brent on the way out. He asks her to call him, and she says okay. I don't think Brent or I are convinced that she'll call. Thank goodness I passed him the cash.

GRACE IS STILL QUIET. She appears to be heavy in thought.

"Hey, do you want to grab a drink?" she asks.

I follow her gaze to the lobby bar. I want to say no and make up a lie about having a meeting later today, but I've already met my daily quota of lies.

"Sure, I have time for a drink," I say.

Grace asks the hostess if there's someplace quiet we can sit. I ruffle my brows. I'm a little worried. Maybe she's going to tell me that she did have something to do with the photos of Carter and me. I'm nervous as we follow the young lady with a long swinging ponytail to a quiet spot between two wood panel walls near an electric tabletop fireplace. I order a whisky.

"I'll have one too," Grace says.

I smirk at her. "I learn something new about you all the time."

She closes her eyes. Damn, she looks miserable. "So I'll just say it. I'm the one who got Carter put out of her apartment." She opens her eyes to gauge my reaction.

I go rigid as if she just punched me in the gut. "What the fuck is wrong with you people?"

"I thought I should tell you that before we move forward with Kennedy Creative Interior Designs."

"How can I ever trust you after that?" I shake my hands out of frustration. "Who does this shit?

247

You're messing with people's livelihoods because you're fucking pissed?"

Grace looks at her lap. "I know, but shit, I can't take it back."

"Grace, what are you going to do to me when I piss you off? Because I will piss you off."

"I don't know. Key your car?" She smiles weakly.

I sniff a chuckle. "This is no time for jokes. *Shit.*"

"I know…" She sighs. "Carter and Tyler are always on and off. You know, they rarely have sex, so I don't even know what draws them together."

"Huh?" I'm fucking confused by what that has to do with her fixating on Carter the way she has.

"I went crazy, that's all."

I get control of my anger, confusion, and disgust. "Listen, I've had a lot of sex with a lot of women, and none of it drew me to them." It kills me to say this, but I say, "Carter and Tyler must have something special, and no matter what you do to fuck with it, they're the only ones who can break their bond."

Grace rolls her eyes as if she doesn't want to consider a word of what I just said. "I think Tyler's codependent, and Carter's too lackluster to do anything about it."

I have no idea what she means by that, and frankly, I don't need her to clarify. "How the hell did you get her kicked out of her apartment anyway?"

Grace messes up her thick blond hair. This isn't the first time I've seen her do that when she's frustrated. "While they were on a break and she was working on a project in Barcelona for three months, I stayed at the apartment with Tyler. I left my green dress in one of the drawers."

A waitress brings our whiskeys, and I give her my card and tell her to keep the tab open. We're going to need more than one each after the day we're having.

"And then…?" I say after the waitress leaves.

Grace frowns at the waitress. "She was flirting with you. Did you see that?"

"No, I didn't." I'm getting impatient.

"Well, I'm sitting right here. She doesn't know that we're not together."

"And this is coming from a woman who fucked around with a co-worker's boyfriend?"

Grace narrows an eye at me. "Okay, I deserved that." She pauses as if she's waiting for me to negate that, then she realizes she'd better not hold her breath. "Anyway, I asked Valerie, the manager, to let me into Tyler's apartment to get the dress."

"But Tyler wasn't living there," I say.

"No. He won't take his name off the lease as long as Carter wants to live there."

"And that bothers you?"

"Yes."

"You like Tyler?" I ask.

"I kind of love him."

"And he kind of loves Carter?"

"I think so."

Shit, I have to take a drink.

"Anyway, Valerie and I got to talking. She wanted Carter out too. She said Carter keeps coming on to her husband, Johnny. So I told her I would pay up Tyler's lease if she wanted to kick Carter out. She said she would need a letter from Tyler first, so I wrote one."

"You forged a letter from Tyler?" My head's spinning. There's no fucking way I can have this woman run any part of my company.

Grace puts up her hands as if to steady my reaction. "Listen, I didn't have to tell you any of this. Did I?"

I sigh hard. "No, you didn't."

"That's because I feel like I'm ready to make a new lease on life."

"Just the other day, you dropped your fucking list on my desk and tried to extort me with it."

Grace sighs and takes a drink. "I did that half-heartedly."

I grunt cynically. "What the fuck does that mean?"

She throws her hands up. "You know what? Maybe you're too perfect to know what I mean by making a new lease on life, but I'm not. Something really woke me up here. Matt and I doing crazy shit in the name of love? I just want to prove to myself and you that I can be a different person, that's all."

I sigh and hold up my hand so the waitress can see me. "You want another whisky?" I ask Grace.

"I haven't even started on this one."

The waitress is on the way.

"Finish it," I say.

"But what's the verdict?"

"I know about new leases on life. I'll give you one."

The waitress arrives. "What can I get you?"

Grace slaps her credit card on the table. "Two more whiskeys on me."

The waitress looks at me for corroboration.

"You heard what the crazy lady said," I say, smirking at Grace.

She bursts out laughing. The waitress looks at Grace as if she's insane.

"See? Crazy," I say.

Grace laughs harder.

WEDNESDAY MORNING...

Another day, another wacked employee to deal with. The person I've been waiting for arrives and sits down at his desk. I walk out of my office. I see that Carter's workspace is still empty. It's nine thirty. She's usually one of the first to arrive. I turn my gaze directly across the room to where Matt Franks sits. Strangely enough, our eyes meet. Matt watches me as I walk to his desk.

"Can I see you in my office?" I ask.

He stiffens. "Um, sure."

I wait until he stands. "After you," I say.

I glare at the back of his head. I'm more worried about where Carter is than angry at Matt for pulling a stupid stunt like using doctored photos to get me to fire Carter. I can't help but think that I've crossed a major line by having sex with her. If I kick myself one more time for not keeping it in my pants, then I'd put myself in the hospital.

Matt stops beside a guest chair in front of my desk. I can tell the guy is so scared that he's probably already shit himself.

I sit and get comfortable. "Have a seat."

He hesitates but sits. "I'm sorry, but what's this all about?"

I look him in the eye, and he squirms. "You have no idea why I asked you to come into my office?"

He shakes his head and gulps. "No."

I take the envelope out of my top drawer, open it, and show him the photos. "Do these look familiar to you?"

"Um, no."

I drop the photos in front of him. "Why not? You took them."

Matt shakes his head in shame. Shit, if I weren't so empathetic, I would tell him to pack his things and get the fuck out of my building.

"Why did you do it?" I ask.

His eyes are watery. I hope he doesn't cry. I wouldn't know what to do if a grown man bawled right in front of me.

"I don't know," he says with a sigh. "I was mad at her for…" He clenches his lips.

"Mad at Carter for what?"

"She sort of dicked me around."

"You went through all of this because she dicked you around? Women do shit like that all the time."

He shrugs.

I shake my head and let out a sigh of resolve. "Shit, Matt. You know I have to fire you, right?"

"I don't care. As long as she works here, I don't want to be here."

I can't help feeling sorry for the poor guy. He looks as if he's only in his mid-twenties, and he's already having problems dealing with women.

I rub my top lip, trying to think of what to say to him. "A guy has to be pretty out there to follow a chick and take pictures of her with her boss—and then threaten to expose the boss for fraternization if he doesn't stop fucking her." I watch to see how he reacts.

He blinks as if nothing I said computed. "I wasn't trying to get pictures of you and her. She kept saying that she wasn't fucking around with Tyler, so I wanted proof."

"Was she fucking around with you?"

"She broke it off with me."

"So why the hell did you need proof?"

He looks at me as if that's the hardest question to answer on an IQ test. "But what the fuck? You're the one who's fucking her."

I'm taken aback. "Is that your response to what I just said?"

"Aren't you?" His tone is demanding.

I look him square in the eyes. "No, I am not and never have."

He searches my face for the lie I just told. I know he can't find it. His face turns red as he scratches the back of his neck. "Shit, what the fuck did I do?"

He's doing exactly what I didn't want him to do. He's turned all red and clammy as he wipes his eyes. I get up and close the door so that curious onlookers can't hear him. I learned a long time ago that the glass is soundproof.

I pat Matt's shoulder. "Listen, you're not the first man who has fallen to the wiles of a woman."

"Then what was she doing with you?" he says.

"Carter and I are old friends."

He looks at me with furrowed eyebrows.

"My best friend is her cousin. We're just friends. That's all. We didn't tell anyone because I didn't want people to think that I promoted her because I know her. Just like you, she does fucking good work."

My computer dings. I've just received an email from Carter.

Matt squeezes his head out of frustration. "Shit, I just lost my job. What am I going to do?" He searches my face for the answer.

I open the email, and my mouth falls open. "What the fuck?"

"What is it?" Matt asks.

I cover my dismay so that I can continue to handle this ordeal. "Nothing you need to know. So, Matt, I'm going to have to fire you." Shit, I don't even like the way that sounds.

"You can't give me another chance?"

"Would you give you another chance if you were me?"

He gazes off to think. After a moment, he sighs. "I guess I fucked up."

He and I are still studying each other. I think he senses my ambivalence. I've never had to fire a person other than Grace, and the shit just doesn't sit well with me. Maybe in the future, when I've atoned for all of my sins against Vince, it will, but not yet.

"Matt," I say, "today is your lucky day."

I choose not to fire Matt if he agrees to my stipulations. He has to give me the memory card with the pictures he took, along with the computer he used to download the photos. I'll keep the computer for forty-eight hours, long enough to get it wiped. As long as he has those photos, he has my ass. Hell, keeping him close and not pissing him off is probably smarter than firing him and letting him keep those pictures to use whenever the feeling hits.

13

THE RT SUCCESS STORY

TWO MONTHS LATER...

I'm finishing up a phone interview with the reporter from *MM Magazine*. MM stands for money masters, and they're one of the top financial magazines in the world. I've been stuck in silence for a while, trying to keep my composure.

I clear my throat. "He said that?" I ask again.

"I'm quoting Vincent Adams directly. He said that if it weren't for Robert Tango, A&RT Media wouldn't be the contender that it is today. He said that you built the business model and structure. You hired the right people, and the company took off from there."

Like a good reporter, he's trying to keep my emotions stirred up, and it's working.

"He also said he's not surprised that you made your own company successful so quickly."

I swallow again to take the tightness out of my throat. "I'm flattered."

"Are you? I'm surprised. I thought you two were best friends?"

It's time to lie my ass off in order to save face. "We are."

"Yeah, yeah…" he says.

There's awkward silence. He's waiting for me to fill it.

"Okay… well, thank you, Mr. Tango, for this great interview. It's been inspiring, and I'm sure our readers will think the same."

"You're welcome," I say.

"Oh, one more thing. I heard you're expanding to New York next summer. Is that true?"

I look over at Jim Nelson, my business development officer, sitting on the sofa. He shows me a thumbs-up. We've been waiting for this moment. Any reporter worth his salt, who was fed that information, would bring it up.

I wink at Jim. "Who told you that?"

The reporter chuckles. "I can't reveal my sources."

"Well, you're just going to have to wait and see, aren't you?"

"Is that a yes?"

"If that were true, then that would be in-house knowledge that only four people in this company would know."

'Right... right..." he says. "Well, thanks again, and please be in touch if there's anything that we didn't cover that you feel we should have."

"Will do," I say and end the call.

Jim stands. "He's going to run with it."

"Yes, he is."

He shows me a thumbs-up and shakes his fist victoriously. "Are you coming tonight?"

"I'll be there. I just need a moment."

"Then I'll see you later."

Jim leaves my office. Tonight a group of us, including all of my company officers and chief and principal architects, are getting together to celebrate our story in MM Magazine. The article is about me, but I would have no success without them. Drinks and dinner are on me.

I take my cell phone out of my top desk drawer and contemplate calling Vince. I hadn't given him much thought lately until the reporter mentioned him. I got the message—as far as he's concerned, our friendship is done.

I also had to forget about Carter. Two months ago, the Wednesday after we spent the weekend together, she sent me an email to say that she's quitting and won't be back. She said it was too stressful to work at a place where everyone but me wanted her gone. I responded, *"No hard feelings—be happy."* She responded, *"Likewise."*

I had a severe pain in my chest for at least three days after that. If I weren't so busy building a company and a new house, then I swear I would've accepted that I had a broken heart. Sometimes I still miss Carter. I know she's still in touch with Tyler, but he and I don't talk about her.

I'm staring at my phone, willing myself to pick it up and call Vince. He'll probably let it go straight to voicemail, but I can't let the possible rejection detour me. I swipe the phone off the table, and just before I plug in Vince's number, it rings.

I gasp. Shit. It's him. "Hello." I sound desperate, but I don't care.

"Hey, Rob, how are you?" He sounds happy.

"I'm good. How are you?" I sit up and look around, wondering if anybody is noticing that the one thing I wanted most to happen is occurring right at this second.

"Actually, it can't get much better."

"That's good."

"And congratulations on *MM*. I'm proud of you, brother."

He called me brother. "Thanks." My voice cracks. "That means a lot coming from you."

"So…" he says, changing his tone. "I've been thinking. Maggie and I are finally tying the knot. And um, there's only one best man for me."

Energy rises from my feet to my head, and I shoot out of my seat like a rocket. "Are you asking me to be your best man?"

"I am," he says.

"Yes." My tone is definite.

"And I'm sorry for treating you like an ass, brother."

"No, don't you apologize. The shit I've done to you, I'm lucky you're talking to me now."

This is what reward looks like. Both Grace and Matt have been working out perfectly. Instead of judgment, I utilized empathy. I may have fucked Carter, but I didn't fuck her over. And now, the one fucking thing that I wanted in this whole fucking world has happened.

Vince is silent, then he clears his throat. "Well, the wedding is going to be in Colorado."

I clear my throat. "Oh yeah?"

"Maggie doesn't like it, but she's willing to go through with it if it makes me happy."

"Your sisters are going to drive her nuts," I say.

"They already are."

I chuckle and sit back down. It seems I've garnered a lot of attention from my staff. Zoe and everybody else are watching me curiously. I wink and smile at Zoe. She blushes. I have to stop doing that. The women in the company are getting more aggressive about pursuing me. But there's only one woman I've been dreaming of fucking, and she's all the way in Washington, DC.

Vince and I talk some more about what I've been doing for RT Creative, business-wise. He gets me caught up on A&Rt Media.

"How in the hell did you get both of your initials in A&Rt, and I only got A for Adams?" Vince says.

I laugh. "Remember we tried Vt&Rt and A&T, but that sounded too much like the phone company."

Vince laughs. We're talking to each other like old times. Hours pass, and we're still on the telephone. Before I hang up three hours later, I promise to fly out to Colorado next week for one week.

Matt Franks knocks on my door. I wave him in.

"Ready, boss? You're our designated driver."

I hop to my feet. "I'm ready!" I grab my coat, smiling like a circus clown. Life couldn't be better.

CARTER

Carter moved to Washington, DC, two months earlier, and it had been so cold that she could barely stand it. She had hoped she would hate Metropolis Architecture and go crawling back to Robert to ask for her old job back, but that hadn't been the case. She loved DC. The weather was forty degrees colder than it was in California, but the general spirit of the city couldn't agree with her more. She had friends in DC. They'd all tried to hook her up, so she had been on many dates. But with all of the nice and professional men she'd met, none of them could make her stop thinking about Robert Tango. The things he'd done to her body when they made love… the depth of their kissing and touching…

Since moving to DC, she had let her hair grow

out and returned to her original ash-blond. She sold her motorcycle and bought a small fuel-efficient car for weekend drives to Virginia, Maryland, Massachusetts, New York, and everywhere in between. The east coast had some of the best real estate on Earth, and she visited so many construction sites that her mind stayed full of ideas for her new clients. She didn't live far from work, so on the weekdays, she caught the bus to the office.

Tonight she had a date with another guy her new friend Janelle had set her up with. Most of her girlfriends were her age and already married. They had careers but were planning on popping out the babies as soon as they turned thirty. Carter thought of them as nice women but from an alien planet called Crazyville. Regardless, she couldn't sit in the house every night, so she spent time in the best bars, restaurants, and nightclubs on the planet. DC had every scene a person could look for—jazz, Latin, Caribbean, rock, pop, and some spots had them all.

She sat at her desk waiting for her date to arrive. He was supposed to pick her up from the office at six thirty. Three of her girlfriends had stayed behind to get a glimpse of him. Janelle, the one who had set her up, said he was a solid ten, and the other women wanted to see if that was true.

The phone in Carter's purse rang. She scrambled to open her purse and answer it. At first she thought the guy was calling to cancel on her. It was snowing out, but he was only coming from Georgetown to Dupont Circle.

"Hello," Carter said without looking at the name on the screen.

"Carter?"

Shit, it was Allie. "Allie, what do you want?"

"I want you to get on an airplane and come to Denver next week. Did you get the invitation?"

"For Vince's wedding, yes. But I can't leave early. I have work."

"You have work unlike me?"

Carter sighed and rolled her eyes. "That's not what I said."

"Don't you love your cousin, Carter?"

"Don't pull that crap."

"What crap?" a man with a smooth tone said.

Carter jumped and looked behind her. Her mouth dropped open. There stood a tall, dark, and handsome specimen of a man.

"Allie, I have to go," Carter said.

"Carter, Monday? Please."

Carter noted that her cousin had resorted to shameless pleading.

The guy smiled. Janelle had said his name was Rico.

Carter raised a finger and mouthed, "One second."

Rico raised a hand and mouthed, "I'm fine."

"You can't stand us up this time," Allie said. "Vince's girlfriend is being a bitch. He's convinced her to give us three spots for bridesmaids, and Lexie backed out, so now it's only Allie, you, and me."

Rico was looking right at Carter, and for some reason, she was embarrassed to have that conversation in front of him. She cradled the phone to her ear and whispered, "I haven't agreed to anything. And isn't she the bride?"

"That remains to be seen."

"What does that mean?"

"It's not over until they both say I do."

Suddenly Carter felt so bad for Vince. He had the worst meddling sisters.

"I was thinking that maybe I can get Rob on our side," Allie said.

"Robert Tango?" Carter looked at Rico as if he had been privy to some deep dark secret she was keeping from him.

"Your old boss, yes."

"He's going to be there?"

"Vince said he was the best man."

Rico smiled at her. Her mind replaced his face with Robert Tango's. Gosh, she missed him. "Okay. I'll be there."

"Yeah?" Allie sounded excited.

"Monday?"

"Morning. Monday morning."

"Okay. Now I have to go."

Allie hung up without saying good-bye. Carter shook her head and brought the phone down from her ear.

"That sounded intense," Rico said, wearing a sexy grin.

"It was."

"Are you ready to eat dinner?"

Surprisingly, Carter had to think about it. Robert Tango would be attending Vince's wedding. She remembered that that was all he had wanted— to restore his friendship with Vince.

"Sure," Carter said. There was nothing wrong with spending an evening with a nice-looking guy even if she was thinking about Robert all night. "I'll get my coat."

He waited as she got ready to leave. When Rico

and Carter walked past her new colleagues and friends, the girls gave her a thumbs-up. She was smiling so hard, and they had no idea of the real reason why. None of them. Carter knew that the next time she made love, it would be to the man she had always loved.

ABOUT THE AUTHOR

For more information:
zlarkadiebooks.com
contact@zlarkadiebooks.com